# SWARM OF FIRE

## AN IAN DEX SUPERNATURAL THRILLER BOOK 5

### JOHN P. LOGSDON
### CHRISTOPHER P. YOUNG

CRIMSON MYTH
PRESS

**Published by**: Crimson Myth Press (www.CrimsonMyth.com)

**Cover art:** Jake Logsdon (www.JakeLogsdon.com)

**Thanks to TEAM ASS!**
*Advanced **S**tory **S**quad*

This is the first line of readers of the series. Their job is to help me keep things in check and also to make sure I'm not doing anything way off base in the various story locations!

(listed in alphabetical order by first name)

Adam Saunders-Pederick
Bennah Phelps
Debbie Tily
Hal Bass
Helen Saunders-Pederick
John Debnam
Larry Diaz Tushman
Marie McCraney
Mike Helas
Natalie Fallon
Noah Sturdevant
Paulette Kilgore
Penny Campbell-Myhill
Scott Reid
Tehrene Hart

**Thanks to Team DAMN**
*Demented And Magnificently Naughty*

This crew is the second line of readers who get the final draft of the story, report any issues they find, and do their best to inflate my fragile ego.

(listed in alphabetical order by first name)

Adam Goldstein, Amy Robertson, Bonnie Dale Keck, Carolyn Fielding, Carolyn Jean Evans, Charlotte Webby, Dan Sippel, David Botell, Denise King, Helen Day, Ian Nick Tarry, Jacky Oxley, Jamie Gray, Jan Gray, Jim Stoltz, Jodie Stackowiak, Kate Smith, Kathleen Portig, Kathryne Nield, Kevin Frost, Laura Stoddart, Mark Brown, Mary Letton, MaryAnn Sims, Megan McBrien, Michelle Reopel, Myles Mary Cohen, Pete Sandry, Ruth Nield, Sandee Lloyd, Sara Pateman, Steve Woofie Widner.

# CHAPTER 1

*T*his was going to be uncomfortable.

While Dr. Vernon and I had only had one sexual encounter, it was clear that the psychiatrist for the Las Vegas Paranormal Police Department (PPD) was hungry for another. I knew this because she had her hair down, her glasses off, and the top few buttons of her blouse undone. It was enough to see that she wasn't wearing a bra.

I gulped.

"Tell me about your last mission, Officer Dex," she said seductively as her amethyst eyes flashed against her dark-skinned cheeks. She was pushing me toward the couch. "Don't spare any details."

Normally, I'd be jumping at the chance to provide her with some personal fun-time, but I was now in a committed relationship with my partner, Rachel Cress, and I really didn't want it to get destroyed. Rachel was the type who would give me a penicure, which was like a pedicure for your pecker, if she found me cheating on her. But I was the loyal type anyway. I *never* cheated on anyone, assuming we had an agreement in place. I would leave them first.

*"What are you waiting for, pal?"* The Admiral asked. *"This chick is smokin' hot!"*

The Admiral was the name Rachel had given to my dick because he tended to stand at attention a lot. I hadn't heard from him in a very long time, but that's because he'd had nothing to say. When I was consistently active in the sack, he remained pleasantly silent. Whenever I was in a relationship, though...not so much. Now that Rachel and I were together again, he was bound to be more talkative. Eventually—if it was anything like that last time Rachel and I dated—he'd shut up, but for now I was going to have to deal with him.

*"Quiet, you,"* I replied. *"We're in a relationship now, remember?"*

I slid away from Dr. Vernon. "I can't do that again with you, I'm afraid."

"There's no reason to be afraid," she said with one eyebrow up. Then she squinted. "Actually, I thought you got turned on when you *were* afraid."

I jolted at that. "Only if it's play and there's a safe word involved."

"Fine with me." She licked her lips. "What would you like your safe word to be?"

The Admiral said, *"I vote for 'Don't Stop!'"*

*"That's two words, idiot."*

*"Semantics."*

"Look, Doc," I backed off further, "I'm saying that I *can't* have sex with you."

Her face turned from lust to concern. This didn't usually happen to me until after I'd had sex with someone.

"Were you injured or something?"

*"Mentally."*

"No, nothing like that," I replied, ignoring The Admiral. "It's just that Rachel is back on the force and we're a couple again."

"Oh, I see," she said, immediately buttoning up her shirt. "This is very interesting."

*"Dude, what are you doing? The breasts are going away!"*

I felt bad because I knew the doctor had to be embarrassed, but what choice did I have? I had to tell her before things got too far. Granted, it probably would have been nice of me to send her an email or something so we could have avoided a scene like this entirely.

Oops.

"Listen, Doc," I uttered, "I don't want you to think that—"

"Oh, don't worry about me," she said as she put on her glasses and snapped up her journal. "Getting into the weeds of someone's psychology is far more interesting to me than a quick roll in the hay."

"Quick?"

*"I'm okay with quick."*

"You know what I mean," she said, motioning for me to get on the couch. "I have a number of questions for you regarding this relationship between you and Rachel, but first I need to thumb back through your history in order to recall everything that's happened between you two. It's been a while, you know."

Oh boy.

"Sit, sit," she commanded while pointing at the couch. "This will just take a minute."

*"You're not even a man,"* The Admiral grumbled.

*"I'd argue I'm more of a man for not boning her."*

*"Whatever you say, Sally."*

Finally, I sat on the couch.

Nothing good could come from this. I knew it and I was sure Dr. Vernon knew it.

"Ah yes," she said while nodding. "I remember this." The pages were flipping faster and faster. "Oh yeah, that's right. Okay, okay. All set now."

It was in moments like these that I wished I'd gone to The Three Angry Wives Pub *before* starting my day.

*"If you'd have done that, we might be getting laid right now."*

*"We literally got laid three times this morning,"* I argued.

*"What's your point?"*

"Now," Dr. Vernon started, acting far more excited than I considered appropriate, "you two fought a lot when you were dating, right?"

"We fight a lot regardless of whether we're dating or not," I answered.

"Exactly. So what would make you want to get back into a situation like that?"

I frowned at the question.

This was honestly a level of introspection that I hadn't considered going into. Was this because I wanted to avoid what I thought to be the answer? Or maybe it was a case of me not really knowing why in the first place?

"Well…uh…"

"Is it love?" she asked pointedly.

"I…uh…"

It had to be, right? I'd spent a long time with Rachel by my side. We fought together, laughed together, yelled at each other, called each other names…. Hell, if anyone didn't know us better, they'd have thought we'd been married for years.

*"Oh, brother. He's completely gone. We'll never see a fresh pair of breasts again. Just the same ones over and over and over…"*

"Yes?" I said with trepidation, shutting down the droning of The Admiral.

Her pen was hovering over the page. "You're not sure?"

"I'm…" I coughed.

There was more than one type of love. You had friendship love, dependency love, familiarity love…and then you had the big LOVE type of love.

Which one did Rachel and I share? And did we both feel the same kind?

"I definitely love her," I said finally, "but…" Again, I trailed off.

"You don't know if you're *in love* with her," finished Dr. Vernon.

I looked away, not sure how to respond to that.

Nearly everything in my being said I *was* in love with Rachel.

Nearly.

There was a sliver of my psyche that wasn't positive.

*"Yeah, that's me, dumbass."*

*"Will you* please *shut the fuck up?"*

"Do you want to know what I think?" Dr. Vernon asked, closing her book and leaning forward.

"Honestly, yes."

She nodded.

"I think you're in a relationship with each other because nobody else in this world can understand you the way she can. The same goes for her. There is no one anywhere who knows Rachel Cress the way you do."

"Okay?"

"You're safe with each other," she finalized.

"Then why do we fight all the time?"

"Because, Ian," she reiterated while giving me a strong look, "you are *safe* with each other."

"You already said that."

Dr. Vernon leaned back and crossed her legs as she chewed on her lip. She began tapping her pen on the journal, clearly thinking things through.

*"Come on, man. You have to admit she looks seriously boneable when she does that chewing-on-her-lip thing."*

I ignored…well, *me*, I suppose.

5

"Okay," she said after a minute, "do you fight with any of the other officers the way you do with Rachel?"

"No."

"Why is that?"

"Because they're not my partners," I answered. "I gave grief to Harvey for a bit, but even that wasn't like Rachel. Of course, we were only partners for a short time."

"Could you ever see yourself arguing with Harvey like you do with Rachel?"

I couldn't. It just wasn't the same thing.

"No," I admitted.

"And what about Serena, Jasmine, Felicia, Griff, Chuck, Turbo, or even Lydia? Could you imagine arguing with them the same as you do with Rachel?"

I shook my head slowly.

She was clearly on to something here.

I glanced up and winced slightly. "So am I *in love* with Rachel?"

"I can't answer that question for you," Dr. Vernon replied, "but I will say that my guess is you're not." She opened up her book and jotted something down. "My bet is that you're in love with the security of having someone with you who understands all of your idiosyncrasies in the way that you understand hers."

"I fail to see the difference."

She peered over the rims of her glasses.

"Do you want to buy Rachel flowers, take her to a movie, take her out for a nice romantic dinner, travel with her to Venice, and spend time strolling with her on the French Riviera?"

"She'd kick my ass if I gave her flowers," I replied.

"You get my point." Dr. Vernon didn't like it when I got too particular about her advice. "You're not romantically in love with her, Ian. You're in love with the fact that you have someone who shares your misery. She's the closest thing you have to someone in this world who understands what it means to be an amalgamite."

"She's not an amal—"

"No, but she's been around you longer than anyone else. She *understands*." Dr. Vernon leaned forward again. *"That* is what you are in love with, in my opinion."

"Oh."

CHAPTER 2

*I* walked outside, feeling more confused than refreshed. Rachel was leaning back on my red Aston Martin, looking as smoking hot as ever.

She had her blond hair down today, which was a rarity. Usually she kept it up in a braid because she hated it getting in her face. I used to pester her to just cut it short but when I saw it framing her perfect face like this, it made me glad she rarely listened to me.

"How'd it go?" she asked as I approached the car. "You look like you're deep in thought."

"Hmmm? Oh, yeah. Just going over what the doc and I talked about."

"Did she try to jump your bones?" she asked.

*"Yes, but he was too much of a pussy to—"*

*"Enough from you!"*

Rachel had known me long enough to tell when I'd been laid, so she was well aware that I hadn't done anything.

"Yeah," I answered thoughtfully. "I told her 'no,' of course."

"I can see that." Then she crossed her arms. "Is that why

you're off in la-la land? Irritated that you couldn't knock boots with her?"

I just gave her a look that signified I wasn't planning on dignifying that question with a response. Fact was that boning Dr. Vernon *had been* fun, especially because I got to use that *Time* skill that Gabe the vampire had given me. Of course he hadn't told me at that point that there were only three uses of that particular skill available to me. But watching a woman in the throes of orgasmic pleasure in slow motion while she's riding you is something every fella should experience.

My face must have gone serene because Rachel slapped my shoulder.

"Perv."

I shook myself back to the moment.

"Sorry," I said. "Anyway, it was just an enlightening conversation, is all. She made me think about things I hadn't considered before."

Her eyes narrowed. "Such as?"

This was one of those fork-in-the-road moments you hear about. If I chose to go left and made up something, the night would go smoothly and all would be well. If I chose to go right, though, things would be tense and Rachel would be fuming at me.

Sadly, I was never one to take the easy road.

"Do you love me?" I asked while putting my hands on her shoulders.

Her face turned a nice shade of pale.

"I...what?"

"Do you love me?"

"Yeah..." She looked very confused. "I guess."

"You guess?"

"Well, you know..."

Her eyes were darting about, which indicated she was

feeling now the same way I'd felt when Dr. Vernon was giving me the third degree. It was easy to just accept that all was great between you and your significant other, but it was something else entirely to be forced to really evaluate things.

There was genuine fear in Rachel's eyes.

"Dr. Vernon doesn't think you do," I said as gently as I could.

Rachel's eyes shot open.

"Who the fuck is she to decide who I love and don't love?" she exclaimed as she started toward the building. "Bitch better be hungry 'cause I'm about to shove my fist down her throat."

I caught up and got in her way.

"Wait, wait, wait," I said, fighting to calm her down. "She said the same about me."

Rachel stopped.

"What?"

"She thinks that our love is nothing but familiarity or something." I was trying to remember her exact words, but I couldn't, even though they were just at the end of the previous chapter. "Basically, you and I have been together so long and have been through so much, we share a bond that we don't have with anyone else."

"Sounds like love to me," Rachel challenged.

"And it *is*," I concurred. "A form of love, anyway. But are we actually *in* love?"

That ended her fuming. Now she appeared more like she'd just been slapped.

She looked me in the eye.

"How would I know?"

"Do you want to buy me flowers?" I asked.

"What?"

"Sorry...uh...I mean, do you see yourself doing things with me outside of work?"

JOHN P. LOGSDON & CHRISTOPHER P. YOUNG

Rachel grunted. "We just spent the last three days boning in every room of your house, Ian."

Ah, the memories. That was one hell of a weekend. Ever since we'd returned from London, Rachel and I had been going at it like bunnies. Seriously, I didn't even have this much sex when I paid for it.

But that's not what I was asking her about.

"I'm talking about things like holding hands while walking around the French Rivera."

She grimaced at me and gave me a once-over.

"How close did you and Harvey get to each other when I was gone?"

I sighed and gave her a sad smile.

"Anyway," I said, "that's the discussion we had. It's just making me think." I put my hand out and pushed the hair out of her face. "Maybe you should think about it some, too."

Before she had a chance to respond, Lydia, our Artificial Intelligence dispatcher, called through the connector.

"*Ian, honey,*" she said in her flirty way, "*we have a disturbance down at Harrah's. Seems there are three ape-like creatures terrorizing the patrons.*"

"*Apes?*" I asked as Rachel shrugged.

Lydia was broadcasting to both Rachel and me, based upon the readings from my connector. This was a fantastic device that all Paranormal Police Department officers had embedded in their brains. It allowed us to communicate without the need for speaking aloud. We could target individuals or open to groups, as well, which was quite useful depending on the circumstances.

"*Technically,*" Lydia replied, "*there is a Bigfoot, an abominable snowman, and a swamp ape.*"

Rachel and I shared a "what the fuck?" moment.

"*Okay,*" I said slowly. "*Are the other officers on their way?*"

"*No, sugar,*" she replied, "*they're all dealing with a different* disturbance on the Old Strip. It seems a couple of vampires decided to go feeding."

"We've almost got this locked down, Chief," Officer Jasmine Katrell said through the connector, interrupting our conversation. "We'll have things under control soon enough and then we'll meet you at Harrah's."

"Roger that," I said, going to open the door for Rachel.

She just looked me up and down like I was nuts to be treating her with a hint of chivalry. Then she shrugged and got in.

I rolled my eyes, shut the door, and walked to the other side of the car.

"This ought to be a fun night," I mumbled as I prepared to find Bigfoot.

CHAPTER 3

The front of Harrah's was awash with a crowd and a bunch of security guards. There were also standard cops in the area. Everyone looked pretty damned baffled by what was going on.

Rachel and I got out and walked up to find there were indeed three very large, very hairy beasts standing there.

They were growling and swiping their gigantic hands at people.

Officers and civilians alike were asking each other if this was some kind of show that the casino was running. The security guards were asking each other, too, but it was clear they weren't clued in on anything. That made it obvious that this wasn't a planned event. Management wouldn't spring something like this on their security folks. It was too dangerous.

"*Thoughts?*" asked Rachel through the connector.

"*My guess is we're looking at something that's not supposed to be here.*"

She inclined her head at me. "*And here I was thinking that it was only Harvey who had pretended he was Sherlock Holmes.*"

15

*"Har har,"* I replied.

At this moment, I kind of missed Harvey. Yes, he was a big oaf who was somewhat misguided in the realm of police work, but he was a decent enough guy. Plus, with him as my partner, I wouldn't have been having thoughts over whether or not to buy him flowers.

"Let's get up there," I said aloud and then started pushing through the crowd. "If nothing else, we can get a bead on what we're dealing with."

"Watch it, pal," said a burly guy who was wearing a Hawaiian shirt.

"Sorry," I replied, giving him a fake smile.

I then pulled out my wallet and flipped my badge at a security guard who was watching me.

His eyes lit up, telling me he was more than happy to see members of the Las Vegas PPD arrive.

While most of the people who worked at the casinos were normals, they were in-the-know regarding supernaturals. This was necessary because a lot of the owners and people in high positions were supers. Plus, there were special areas in each casino where supers could hang out and do stuff without the worry of being spotted by normals. Well, those who were not in-the-know, anyway.

The guard snagged a Vegas cop by the arm and pointed at me.

In turn, the cop started clearing a path for us until we got to the front where the three massive apes were standing.

They were all ridiculously tall, coming in at around eight to nine feet in height. The first one had brown hair, a sunken forehead, and big round eyes. I looked at his feet and found that they were ginormous, which I supposed made sense. The second one was covered in white fur, had a pinkish face, and large blue eyes. It also had a nice row of teeth that it was busily showing the crowd. The last one was more hunched over. It had matted brown and black hair that looked somewhat sticky. They all smelled horrible, but I had a feeling that the last one in line was the cause of the majority of fumes.

"Officers," I said with a nod to the small group of cops and guards, "I'm Chief Ian Dex and this is Officer Rachel Cress. What have we got here?"

"Three apes," said the security guard while pointing.

"Thank you," I replied evenly. "Have they injured anyone?"

"Not that I'm aware of," the guard replied, "but they've been roaring at people a lot and putting the scare into them."

I nodded at him as Rachel stepped over and stood just out of arm's reach of the brown one. It growled at her as its face creased angrily. Rachel didn't seem bothered.

"Have you tried anything to get them to leave?" I asked.

Honestly, I was paying more attention to the fact that I may have to jump in and help Rachel at any moment.

"Like what?" said one of the cops. "Those things are huge. We put in a call to your office and have been waiting for you to arrive ever since. This is your jurisdiction, pal. Not ours. We're doing all we can to keep people back from these things."

"Fair enough," I said, pushing past them and over to Rachel. "Those are some big apes."

"Yep."

"*Lydia,*" I said through the connector, "*has Paula Rose been notified about this yet?*"

Paula was the head of The Spin, a company who had the unfortunate job of putting a public relations spin on any supernatural activity that affected the normal populace. Basically, she spun the line that there were constantly new shows and attractions happening in Vegas all the time. She

JOHN P. LOGSDON & CHRISTOPHER P. YOUNG

rather despised that incessant copout, but now and then she'd land a nice storyline that put extra coin in her pocket.

But Paula was also one of my ex-girlfriends, and seeing her wasn't exactly a highlight for me. She harbored a fair bit of resentment toward me since I'd broken up with her. In my defense, it was either I broke up with her or I cheated on her. Again, I'm not the cheating type.

"*No, lover,*" Lydia answered. "*I only contact her when you tell me it's okay.*"

"*Please put in a call,*" I said with some effort. "*She's going to need to see this.*"

# CHAPTER 4

*M*y first thought was just to leave the beasts alone. I mean, who knows, maybe they were just here to play some slots.

Okay, even I thought that was a stupid thought.

But the fact was that they weren't actually harming anyone. They were growling and swiping, but nobody had been hurt yet. Terrorizing, sure, but not attacking. For all I knew, this was some crazy promotional stunt done by an up-and-coming magician or something.

And that's when a drunk college kid decided to test the waters.

He darted past me and Rachel, jumped up and swung at the abominable snowman, missed, and ended up getting backhanded, which sent him flying into the crowd.

Now, to be fair, the kid had it coming. I would have backhanded him too.

Unfortunately, his little stunt caused the beasties to take a menacing step forward while their growls increased and their fangs became more pronounced.

I wasn't a fan of blowing away naughties in front of a

bunch of normals, but sometimes you had to do what you had to do. Besides, this was the kind of thing Paula Rose was paid to deal with. We couldn't keep the normals in the dark all of the time, sadly.

I whipped out my .50 caliber Desert Eagle handgun, which I lovingly named "Boomy," and pointed it at the chest of Bigfoot. Rachel's hands were aglow, letting me know her magic was building up and ready to be unleashed.

*"Guys,"* I said through the connector to the rest of my crew, *"I know you're in the middle of stopping vampires from feeding on people at the Old Strip, but I just wanted to let you know that these massive apes have decided to take things to the next level."*

*"Wrapped up the vampires, Chief,"* Jasmine replied. *"We'll be over as soon as we can."*

*"I'm nearby,"* Officer Serena Buchanan, our forensics and part-time healer announced. *"I'll be right there."*

*"Great."*

Based on the size of these things we were facing, having a little of her healing power about now would be great. Every branch of the PPD had at least one healer on board. They took a different track than standard officers so they could spend less time causing harm and more time helping those who were harmed. They were also good at creating healing and energy potions. Needless to say, we were highly protective of officers like Serena.

With a roar, Bigfoot decided to be the first to attack. He leaped forward with the grace of an animal that at that size he really shouldn't have. It was actually somewhat mesmerizing to the point of being beautiful.

But I shot him anyway.

The breaker bullet knocked a massive hole directly through his chest, throwing scatterings of material everywhere.

He staggered and put his hand to his chest while giving me a look of utter shock. Then his brow tightened and the anger in his eyes intensified. It wasn't a fun experience to be the focus of his stare.

When he pulled his hand away from his chest, I saw that the hole had completely closed up.

"What the shit?" I screeched as the crash of ice lightning struck the abominable snowman directly on top of his head, causing me to leap. "Damn it, Rachel! Can you warn me before you do that?"

"Nope."

Another bolt struck Bigfoot and ricocheted over to hit the swamp ape.

All three of them roared in response and I unloaded mayhem at them.

"Shoot!" I screamed at the cops, who were transfixed at the scene before them. "Fire your weapons, you fucking idiots!"

Within seconds, bullets were zipping into the apes like mad.

They were growling, yelping, slapping at their flesh, and doing all they could to dodge our onslaught.

The crowd was getting into things, cheering and whistling. To them, this was probably the best show they'd seen since getting here. Honestly, if I had been in their shoes, I would have thought this was pretty incredible, too. But being that I *wasn't* in their shoes, I was shaking like a leaf.

"*What the hell are these things?*" I said to Rachel through the connector.

"*No idea,*" she replied. "*Immortal Bigfoots is my guess.*"

"*Bigfoots?*" I said between magazine exchanges. "*Wouldn't that be Bigfeet?*"

"*Doubt it.*"

"*Guys,*" Serena called out, "*I'm here. What can I do?*"

I glanced over and saw her amazing body bouncing flawlessly as she ran up the sidewalk. She was a vampire who had all the right curves. Honestly, even the succubus community envied the hotness of Serena Buchanan.

That made me wonder if Bigfoot and his pals thought vampire chicks were hot.

Okay, another dumb thought.

*"I'm not sure,"* I replied. *"These things are healing pretty damn quick, and I don't know why."*

*"What are you hitting them with, Rachel?"*

*"Ice bolts,"* Rachel answered after unleashing another. *"I want to try ice storms, but there are too many people here."*

*"And we've put a buttload of bullets into them since the shit hit the fan,"* I chimed in. *"Blows a hole right through them and it closes back up like it's nothing."*

Serena moved in a wide arc around the apes as we continued shooting at them. She was clearly trying to stay out of the line of fire, but it looked like she was also planning to get pretty near to the damn things.

*"What are you doing?"* I asked, worried for her safety.

*"I have to see what they're made of."*

I scoffed at her. *"Sorry?"*

Serena ignored the question and dived to the ground behind the creatures. She scooped up something before crawling backward, away from them. Then she began studying whatever she'd picked up as we continued blasting away. At one point it looked like she even tasted it.

Ew.

*"This is pixie dust,"* Serena yelped as her head snapped up. *"These things aren't real."*

## CHAPTER 5

*B*igfoot caught me on the shoulder with a vicious swipe, throwing me to the ground while ripping a hole in my suit.

Damn it.

*"Sure as fuck seem real,"* I said while firing up at the monster from my back. *"They seem very real."*

*"You need to melt the dust, Rachel,"* Serena stated. *"Ice isn't going to work. Use heat lightning."*

*"Right,"* Rachel replied. *"Cover me!"*

I scrambled back up and started firing Boomy with deadly accuracy. Well, it would have been deadly against things that didn't just heal up like it was nothing. Obviously the bullets were still hurting them, but there was no killing these bastards with projectiles.

Rachel's hands started glowing bright red as a ball of flame formed. She unleashed it at the swamp ape and it bellowed a blood-curdling scream that nearly made me shit myself. Its right arm and part of its torso looked like it had turned into glass.

The other beasties saw this and immediately went after

Rachel.

"Oh fuck," she choked aloud.

I jumped straight up and to the side until all three ape heads were in a perfect line from my vantage point. The breaker bullet launched from Boomy and ripped through each skull in line, and then cracked against the wall on the outside of the casino.

The apes wailed and grabbed at their heads, giving Rachel enough time to launch a spray of fire at their legs, turning them to glass and freezing them in place.

That should have done the job, but the damn things started doing something neither of us could have expected. They took hunks of their own flesh—or maybe dust?—and began sprinkling it over the glass on their legs. The glass began turning back into skin, or whatever the hell it was.

"Wow," said Rachel with a shocked look that I was wearing as well. "Didn't expect that."

*"Hit their hands and feet,"* suggested Serena. *"If they can't pull their own bodies apart, they can't sprinkle the pixie dust."*

Rachel nodded and a fire ball showed up in her hand in a flash.

Unfortunately, the abominable snowman, who seemed to be the brains of this outfit, smacked her arm just before she launched the attack. The fire ball went straight up toward the clouds and exploded like a nice round of fireworks.

This elicited an "Oooooh" and "Ahhhhh" sequence from the crowd.

Mr. Abominable and the two other apes made the mistake of enjoying the show, too, though. Clearly they found the pretty lights to be just as fascinating as the drunks surrounding us did.

Their mental lapse gave Rachel the time to build up another stream of fire and strike their collective hands with it.

The apes screeched.

Bigfoot kicked me in the chest hard enough that Boomy went flying up in the air and I went barreling back toward the crowd. It hurt my chest, but the guy in the Hawaiian shirt who'd yelled at me earlier broke my fall. Apparently, he'd pushed to the front of the crowd for a better view of the show. Based on how his eyes had rolled up in his head at that moment, I guessed he was watching little birdies instead.

I shook my head and looked over to see that Rachel was also lying in a heap by the crowd.

"All right, you fuckers," I hissed under my breath. "It's one thing to kick me about, but it's quite another to mess with my girl."

As rage welled up inside me, I launched myself at the beasts. I punched, kicked, chopped, rolled, and even head-butted. But all I had accomplished was tiring myself out. The apes didn't seem affected by it at all.

In fact, Mr. Abominable even chuckled a bit before grabbing me by the neck and throwing me at the side of Harrah's.

"Ouch," I said as I finally came to rest on the ground, certain that my head was bleeding.

I'd heal.

"*We've got you covered,*" came the welcome voice of Jasmine as a ball of fire flew over the crowd and struck the abominable snowman square in the chest.

Another flaming orb smacked Bigfoot as well.

All the cops and security guards hit the ground to protect themselves from the incoming flames. The crowd was far enough back not to be affected, and my mages were very good at avoiding normals with their spells. Most of the time anyway.

It only took a few more seconds before Griff, Rachel, and Jasmine had turned these beasts completely into glass.

The crowd was silenced as everyone got back up to look at the apes in their new form.

"*Now what, Serena?*" I said while dragging myself back to my feet.

"*Shoot them.*"

I frowned at her, but she nodded her encouragement.

I grunted. "*Okay.*"

Like someone who'd had far more than his share of booze, I stumbled over to Boomy and picked him up.

Then I pointed at Bigfoot's glass head and pulled the trigger.

It shattered into a million pieces the moment the breaker bullet impacted.

The crowd went nuts.

Frankly, it *had* looked pretty sweet, and I could only imagine them seeing me as the star of this show, though my mages probably appeared pretty badass while they were firing off magical balls of death.

My head began to clear.

"Hey, guys," I said to Officers Felicia Logan and Chuck Taylor, "what say we three use our Desert Eagles on these things to add a little flair?"

They both glanced at me and then smirked.

We looked like the Three Amigos as we shot the living crap out of the massive glass figurines in front of us.

When it was all said and done, the crowd was applauding like mad.

We were a hit.

A major hit.

So this was what it felt like to be on stage at one of the shows here in Vegas. Well, one of the good shows anyway.

It was definitely something I could get used to.

With a wink toward the crowd, I spun Boomy and stuck him back in his holster.

"Show-off," said Rachel with a snort.

"Damn straight," I replied, my smile beaming bright enough that the moon could have taken a holiday. "Damn straight."

Right when my smugness was at full bloom, I heard the sound of a golf clap. It was loud, slow, mocking, and grating on the ears.

I turned toward the sound and found the five-foot-two normal known as Paula Rose.

"Look, everyone," I mumbled, "Paula's here. Yay."

"What the hell do you think you're doing?" she asked as the crowd continued cheering. "These people have no idea what's just happened, you freaking idiot."

I almost got a word out when Rachel stepped up next to me, arms crossed, and stared down at Paula.

"Call him an idiot again," Rachel said in a threateningly sweet voice. "I dare you."

"Excuse me?"

"We're a couple again, Paula," I said, using my hand to motion back and forth between me and Rachel. "You know how she gets a little protective?"

"I *didn't* know," Paula replied, staring daggers at Rachel, "and I don't appreciate the threat, *Officer Cress.*"

Fact was that if Rachel laid a finger on Paula, she'd end up in a Netherworld jail cell, lose her badge, and have to go through Deep Reintegration. Paula, on the other hand, would end up eating through a tube for the rest of her life.

Not worth it.

"Okay, you two," I said, stepping between them, "there's no point in fighting over this. Rachel, I'm good here."

She gave me a dirty look, rolled her eyes, and then stormed away.

Fun.

"Paula," I started, bringing her attention back to me, "you've got a gold mine here."

She blinked. "What?"

"Look at this crowd. They're so into this that I'm guessing we'll be signing autographs."

That'd be cool.

"But this was *real*, Ian," she scolded, hands on hips and everything.

"And they don't know that."

She went to retaliate, but she stopped. I could see the wheels were churning. You could say whatever you wanted about Paula Rose, but you'd be hard pressed to prove she was lacking a nose for business.

"So...hmmm."

"Think about it," I ventured. "You hire on a few pixies to build stuff like this, get a couple of mages to play the part, and pick up some actors within the supernatural community to fire guns." I held up a warning finger. "Just make sure they're using rubber bullets or something."

She was nodding slowly. "We could charge casinos for the draw. We'd make a killing." Then she sighed and gave me a sly look. "Honestly, I caught the end of the little 'show' you did here. You and the other PPD officers *were* amazing."

I raised an eyebrow at her. "Want an autograph?"

"No," Paula answered seriously, "but I would like to meet with your team at our offices to discuss this." She glanced around the area. "I'll have one of my crew come out and put a spin on this using the show angle."

"Okay," I said, feeling a mixture of confusion and excitement as Paula walked away. "*Guys,*" I said through the connector, "*The Spin wants us to meet them at their offices.*"

"*For what?*" asked Rachel.

"*I think we may be taking this little kill-the-pixie-dust-creatures show on the road.*"

# CHAPTER 6

*I*'d been to The Spin a number of times back when I was still dating Paula, but it had been upgraded since then. They used to only have one floor with a few offices. Now they had three floors completely booked out. This was due to the little enterprises that were developed every time Paula picked up a new idea. Those usually came from me. In fact, I'd argue that the "spinning of supernatural events part" of The Spin was now just a little piece of what had originally launched this place.

"Hello, Chief Dex," said Murphy Stone, Paula's producer and right-hand woman as she pushed her purplish-red hair out of her eyes. "It's good to see you again. You're still looking as dapper as ever."

She probably wouldn't have made such a comment had I kept on the jacket that had been ripped by that infernal Bigfoot. Fortunately, I'd learned that it was wise to carry around multiple suits and shoes when working in this business.

"Hi, Murphy," Rachel interjected. "Remember me? Rachel Cress? Ian's significant other?" She then got really

JOHN P. LOGSDON & CHRISTOPHER P. YOUNG

condescending and added, "Anyhoo, we were told to come here to meet with your boss, so how about we get to that, hmmm?"

Rachel had a bit of a jealous streak.

No, that wasn't right.

It was more of a that's-my-property thingy. It was one of the issues we'd dealt with the last time we were dating. Funny how you get amnesia toward certain things like this.

*"I remember it,"* The Admiral chimed in. *"Of course I always thought it was kind of hot when she got all jealous."*

*"You would."*

Murphy raised a baffled eyebrow at Rachel and then waved us to follow her.

*"You don't have to do that, Rachel,"* I said in a direct connection to her.

*"Do what?"*

*"Yell at every woman who comes on to me."*

*"Including Murphy,"* she argued while counting on her fingers, *"that makes one."*

*"You're forgetting your comment to Paula back at Harrah's."*

*"She was hitting on you?"*

*"Well, no..."* She hadn't been. In fact, that was one of the few times Rachel had ever stuck up for me. It was kind of nice, truth be told. *"Okay, sorry. But I remember that you used to do this all the time."*

*"It's not my fault that women hit on you incessantly."*

*"Nor is it mine,"* I argued as we entered the conference room and took our chairs.

*"You could dress less attractively."*

*"Wow,"* I said, giving her a look. Nobody else could hear us, but our body language had to have been giving away the fact that we were fighting. *"Listen, I get hit on a lot. It happens. I have a reputation. You know firsthand why I have a reputation. But you also know that I don't cheat."*

She shuffled in her chair as her eyes tightened.

*"Fine. I'm sorry."*

*"Thank you."*

Paula walked into the room after a couple seconds and headed to the front of the table. She looked like a woman in control. I liked that, but I had to keep a disinterested face on or Rachel would know what was on my mind.

*"Freak,"* she said.

Damn it. *How* could she always tell?

"Thank you for coming," Paula said as she placed her hands on the large conference table. "Obviously you all know why you're here. We saw your little act at Harrah's and I think that we could turn this into a profitable little side business." She stood up and began pointing around the room. "All of you are cops and not actors, but I believe that it would be in our best interest to utilize your rawness as much as we can."

Griff leaned forward and cleared his throat.

"Pardon me," he said in his posh voice, "but while all of this is rather enticing, we can't easily be beholden to a particular schedule. Crime doesn't always present itself at our convenience."

Paula nodded in agreement.

"Well put, Officer Benchley," she agreed. "The good news is that we *can* simply tell casinos that there will be a window of time when the events can occur. We can even have that window span days, if necessary." She smiled. "In other words, we arrive when we arrive."

"They'll go for that?" asked Felicia.

"Assuming the show is like you did tonight, yes." She was rubbing her hands together. "They'll beg to be on the list no matter how long it takes."

It sounded great to me, and my officers *did* seem to be pretty interested, but I also knew that this couldn't last forever. Eventually, we'd get bored or there'd be too much going on with work for us to even get one show in a week. Hell, we *did* get trapped in the Badlands at one point. That alone proved we couldn't always keep to a plan, even at a week's notice.

"I think we can start down a path with you, Paula," I spoke up, "but in the long run you'll have to find supers to act in these roles. We can mentor them and such, of course, but I can't commit the PPD force to a long-running show."

She looked a little disappointed, which seemed to make Rachel look a little happier.

"Well, we'll take what we can get," Paula said finally. "This may only have a few months of life anyway, unless we run it sparingly."

"*Honey pie*," Lydia suddenly said through the connector, "*we have another disturbance down at Circus Circus.*"

"I mean, if we—" Paula started, clearly unable to hear Lydia's call.

I held up a finger to interrupt her.

"Got a call coming in from dispatch," I said. "*Sorry, Lydia, what's the deal?*"

"*Eight foot tall, purple dinosaurs,*" she replied.

"*You're kidding.*"

"*No.*"

I smiled devilishly at this.

"What is it?" asked Paula.

"Get your cameras ready," I instructed as my crew stood up. "There are purple dinosaurs down at Circus Circus."

Dollar signs formed on her irises. "You're shitting me."

"I'm really not."

CHAPTER 7

As we drove to Circus Circus, I decided it was time for Rachel and I to have *the talk*.

I didn't want to do it, but if I didn't we'd end up breaking up again. Of course that would mean that everything could go back to the way it was before.

"We need to talk," I said after we shut the doors and I started the car. "What happened in there between you and Murphy can't happen again."

"Well, if she wasn't all up in your face—"

"That doesn't matter, Rachel," I interrupted. "The fact is that everything is coming back to me now." This had to be the worst part of being involved with someone. "There were always issues on both sides of our relationship, but you getting a major attitude whenever you're dating someone just sucks."

"I don't get a major attitude."

*"You guys should break up. Then we could go see Dr. Vernon again. Oooh, and the valkyries, too. I counted seventy-three breasts when we were down there, you know?"*

*"Seventy-three?"*

*"One of them was partially in the shadows."*

"Rachel, you totally do, and not just with me either. Even when you were going out with that nerd Barry back when I'd just joined the force, you were like that with him, too."

"He wasn't a nerd," she mumbled.

Yes, he was. He was proud to be a nerd, too. He'd worked at Nerds'R'Us or something like that. I don't know. They fixed computers and such, and he was the manager, which meant his name-badge read, "King Nerd."

"The point is that it ruins the fun, Rachel," I said, leaving the Barry discussion out of it. "I'm sorry, but it's true. Straight up, word on the street is that you're becoming pretty unlikeable."

"Who the hell said that?"

I wasn't a squealer. "Just some people I know."

"Yeah?" She slammed back into her seat. "Well, fuck them."

"Don't tempt me," I said with a grin. "Some of them may be pretty—"

Her head snapped toward me and her eyes threatened to glow.

"See?" I pointed at her before finishing my little tease. "That's what I'm talking about. If we weren't dating, you'd just say 'ugh' or call me a 'tool' or something and we'd have a laugh. But with us dating, you take everything too seriously."

She rolled her eyes and put her eyes back on the road.

"Okay, okay," she said with a heavy breath. "I admit that I do get a little riled up when I see someone moving in on my territory. I just can't help it."

*"Don't worry about it, baby. It's hot."*

*"Seriously, shut the living shit up, will you?"*

"I know," I replied after a few moments. "Honestly, I appreciated it when you stepped up to Paula and defended me, though it was probably a little *too* threatening."

"Agreed. I felt kind of bad about that. But I have to hand it to her, she was seconds from being toothless and she didn't budge an inch."

We drove along in silence for a bit as we both thought things through. Obviously we had to work on things together to have a successful relationship. That was just common sense. But we also had to be open and honest. Last time we dated, I held stuff inside. This time I wasn't going to do that.

*"Are you thinking about make-up sex too, or is that just me?"*

I didn't respond to myself this time.

"I'm sorry," she said, sounding like it took some effort to get that out. "I guess I'm not very good at girlfriending."

*"She's right. We should break up and head on back to see the good doc—"*

"Just be the same Rachel you are when we're not dating," I reassured. "That's the person I love hanging out with."

"But I'm always making fun of you."

"Exactly."

"You like that?" she asked.

*"I do."*

"What I like, Rachel, is your sarcasm and directness." I turned into the parking lot of Circus Circus. "Your snark is funny, even when it's directed at me. I also like that you're tough, opinionated, and you're one hell of a mage." I parked and shut off the car. "Plus, you're fantastic in the sack."

"Ugh," she said after a pause. "Tool."

I laughed at that, but the best part was that she did too.

"Oh," I continued, "it's also great that you don't worry about weird shit like flowers and fancy necklaces."

"I like fancy necklaces," she confessed with a fake pout.

The rest of the officers were already running up to where all the action was going on. Paula and her camera crew were right behind them. It was time for another show.

"Are we good?" I asked just as Rachel was about to get out of the car. "We can always talk more later, if you want."

She sniffed and winked at me. "You're such a girl."

*"Can't argue with that."*

"Nice."

CHAPTER 8

*W*hen we got up to the front there were definitely five very purple, very kids-TV-show-looking dinosaurs standing there. Honestly, it was as if a handful of Barney the dinosaurs had started going to Gold's Gym, except for their puny forelimbs.

"I'll be right back," Rachel said.

I nodded and headed over to my crew.

"What do we know?" I asked.

"There are two more of these than there were of those gigantic apes," stated Griff.

"Yeah, and these look like that dinosaur from that TV show back in the nineties," said Chuck. "Always wanted to shoot that damn thing."

"You and about ten million—"

"I have a feeling those teeth are going to be able to shred us pretty easily," Felicia interrupted. She was all business. "I don't care if they're made from pixie dust or not, those things have razors in their mouths."

Serena nodded. "The other worry is that the pixie

37

responsible for these manifestations may be doing his or her best to make this increasingly difficult on us."

"What do you mean?" I asked.

"Well, this *is* the second set of dust-built creatures we've seen already," she pointed out. "Think about the last months, Ian. We've had an uber mage, an uber necromancer, an uber dragon, and you just got back from dealing with an uber wolf."

"What's your point?"

She tilted her head at me as if judging my intellect. I used to get offended whenever someone did this. These days I didn't really care.

"I'm just saying that we shouldn't merely assume that these dinosaurs are going to be as easy to defeat as the apes were."

"You thought they were easy?" I scoffed.

"That's not my point."

"She's right," remarked Jasmine with a slow nod. "It's almost like each time we face one of these uber things, they're testing the waters with us and improving the bad guys based upon what we do." She ran her fingers through her hair. "Shitfaced Fred was the king of that."

And he was. I still recalled dealing with each wave of zombies that old turd had put after us. There'd been one misstep on his part, but that only proved that Serena and Jasmine were correct. These ubers *were* using trial and error to feel out our strengths and weaknesses.

"So, what do you think we should do?"

"I don't know," Serena admitted. "Be careful, I guess."

I sighed at that as I glanced over to see that Rachel was talking with Paula and Murphy, and they were all smiling. That was rather unusual, especially after the confrontations that happened earlier.

Had Rachel apologized?

That'd be new.

"What's going on over there?" asked Jasmine, clearly finding things as interesting as I had.

"I haven't a clue," I answered, feeling like I should be concerned. "I don't even—"

"Huh," Felicia grunted, stepping up. "There aren't any fists flying. That's a good sign."

"It *would* be a grand gesture on her part to bury the proverbial hatchet," stated Griff.

Chuck laughed at that. "I'm surprised she hasn't buried a literal hatchet, if I'm being honest."

We all glanced away as Rachel turned to come back toward us. We knew better than to openly say the things we were saying directly to her. She had a way of making your life hurt when you did that.

Regardless, it sure was nice to see her with a little bounce in her step.

"Okay," Rachel announced when she got close in, "they're rolling."

"*Everything all right?*" I said through a direct connection. "*You seemed to be...having fun.*"

She looked at the dinosaurs and replied, "*Don't dig into it, Ian. I apologized and everything is fine now.*"

"*Wow. I'm—*"

"*Don't dig into it,*" she repeated, giving me the stink-eye.

"*Right.*" I coughed and then gave my crew a quick glance. "Everyone ready to battle Barney and his friends?" I asked aloud.

They all nodded. Chuck's enthusiasm was such that I thought his hat might well fall off.

I took inventory of the crowd that had gathered. My guess was just over fifty people stood there. It wasn't a lot, but it was enough to get the word spreading through the Strip, especially when combined with what had happened with the apes. A few more of these events and people would be jumping in their cars or running the streets to catch an impromptu show.

It was about time to knock their socks off.

This was actually fun.

At least it was until the dinosaurs began to sing.

My crew, along with the crowd, stood transfixed as their booming voices literally harmonized.

> *We'll eat you*
> *You will die*
> *We like the taste of human pie*
> *With a big chomp chomp*
> *We'll enjoy your screams and cries*
> *Then we'll consume your flesh*
> *as you die, die, die!*

"That sounds wrong," noted Jasmine.

"On many levels," agreed Felicia.

"Great voices, though," I said dully as they repeated that same verse from their little dinosaur death song. "Just great."

# CHAPTER 9

*I* cracked my neck from side to side and then stepped powerfully out in front of the dinosaurs.

"Enough of this," I yelled somewhat theatrically. "You are not welcome in this area. If you leave of your own volition, we shall not destroy you. Choose unwisely, though, and wrath will rein free this night!"

"*Dork,*" said Rachel through the connector.

The entire PPD crew laughed.

In response to my announcement, though, the five dinosaurs turned their attention directly at me as their singing stopped. The stuffed-animal-style faces somehow contorted into menacing visages of rage. Obviously, they weren't fond of being interrupted.

"Uh oh," I squeaked a split-second before the one closest to me bashed its head against mine.

It rang my bell so hard that I didn't even realize I'd been thrown a good distance, nearly smacking into the crowd. The damn thing had apparently knocked me out.

The fans loved it.

I sat up and tried to shake away the cobwebs.

Iceballs and ice storms smacked the dinosaurs like a cacophony of dissonant chords. Chuck and Felicia had their Eagles out and they were blasting holes in those damn stuffed beasts like there was no tomorrow.

I knew it was all pixie dust, but the pixie responsible for this was pretty damn talented. He or she would be looking at spending time in prison for these little transgressions, which was kind of a shame, honestly.

The dinosaurs didn't have a chance against my crew now that we knew how to stop the pixie dust, but my mages were being careful not to stop the show too quickly. I was really rather impressed with their restraint. Our normal motto was to go in and destroy everything within seconds of arriving. It made cleanup a little tougher on The Spin and on Portman, our resident morgue chief, but it also nipped naughtiness in the bud. Ultimately, that was our job.

With a bit of effort, I got back up and wobbled over to resume my place in the battle.

One of the dinosaurs snapped at me, but I moved away, brought up Boomy, and blew a nice hole in his head.

He shrieked and jumped back as the next one took his place.

Chuck and Jasmine were going full out with acrobatics. They were diving and firing, leaping through the air, kicking off the walls, and doing every other Cirque du Soleil move they could manage. I'd have to say that they were making me look like a wuss in comparison.

Obviously, I couldn't let that happen.

So I did something incredibly stupid.

Right as one of the dinosaurs opened its maw and prepared to chomp down on my head, I dived forward while spinning, landing directly under it and firing straight up and into its nethers. The beast wasn't anatomically correct, but it was the principle of the thing.

The crowd gasped.

The dino yelped.

A literal buttload of pixie dust dumped out of its ass-region all over my head.

No, it wasn't shit, but the crowd sure bellowed in laughter as if it had been.

I rolled away as fast as I could, sensing that my lower half was in jeopardy. It was. Pain seared through my body as the monster bit into my buttocks like I was a perfectly cooked piece of filet mignon.

"Fuck," I screeched, firing Boomy up at the damn dino like a man possessed.

Chuck pulled me away and Serena put her hands on my ass in an effort to help me heal faster than normal. It felt horrible, yet good, if that makes any sense.

"*Perv,*" Rachel said in a direct connection to me.

I winced-smiled.

Serena's skills were miraculous and I was back up and ready to battle again. This time, though, I was going to be a little smarter about it.

"Thanks, Serena."

"Don't be so careless," she answered back, looking a little worn out from healing me.

"Right," I said, thinking it was about time for this show to end. "Gang, let's knock these things out now."

The dinosaurs backed off and gathered together, looking like they may have had a plan. Too bad they didn't have mages like I did.

Fireballs and streams of heat flew from Griff, Jasmine, and Rachel, eliciting blood-curdling roars from the beasts as they were systematically fused into glass.

Once they were nothing more than sculptures, I stepped out and turned to the crowd.

"How about a round of applause for these mages?" I yelled.

Claps and whistles filled the air until I held up my hands to silence everyone.

The power was sweet.

"You're such an idiot," said Rachel with a laugh.

"I know," I replied before raising my voice dramatically. "And now, the best gunslingers in all of Vegas will show you what happens when you mess with the Vegas Strip."

As one, Chuck, Felicia, and I spun back toward the glass dinosaurs. We whipped forth our Desert Eagles, spun them around expertly, and unleashed fury.

Glass blew out in chunks, hitting the side of Circus Circus, smashing on the ground, or going straight up at such a height that we could blow them right out of the air.

But then a flash of smoke erupted, taking us all by surprise.

"What was that?" I asked.

There was no answer, until the fog began to clear.

That's when we noticed that there were five bodies lying on the ground where the dinosaurs had been. There was blood pooling all around them.

The crowd went insane, thinking that this was part of the show.

It wasn't.

"Those are normals," Jasmine said. "Very dead normals."

"We just killed them," whispered Chuck.

I just stared in disbelief.

"Shit."

# CHAPTER 10

We stood staring at the fallen normals as the sound of the world faded into the background. It was one thing to have a normal die as collateral damage, and technically this was exactly what had happened, but the bullets that had ripped through these five innocents belonged to the PPD.

My officers and I killed them.

The crowd was clamoring for autographs, asking when the next show was going to be held, and generally cheering. They had no idea what had really just happened.

"What have we done?" whispered Jasmine as her mouth hung open.

I put my hand on her shoulder, knowing she was quite sensitive about these kinds of things. I wasn't exactly thrilled about it myself. These people didn't deserve their fate.

"It wasn't our fault," I said, trying to console my entire team. "There was no way we could have known there were normals inside of those damn things."

Paula had Murphy shut down production. They looked to be in as much shock as us. There was no clean way to spin this. *"Five normals were killed today by the Paranormal Police Department in downtown Vegas. They had been locked up inside of purple dinosaurs that were made out of pixie dust."* That was a front page news story, not a spin.

"I'll deal with Paula and Murphy," I said heavily.

"No," Rachel stated, grabbing me by the arm. "Let me do it."

I gave her a firm look, but I sensed that she really wanted to do this.

With a nod, I moved out of the way.

*"Lydia,"* I called through the connector, *"we're going to need Portman down here. There are a few normals who died and I don't want them picked up by a regular ambulance."*

*"Are you okay, sugar?"* she asked, sounding worried.

*"We're all a bit shaken up, but none of us were injured badly."*

*"Good."*

I walked over and knelt down to look at each of the faces. They appeared to be about college age. Three young men and two young women, all in the prime of their lives.

"Damn it," I raged as quietly as I could manage. "This is definitely the work of a fucking uber."

"Agreed," stated Griff.

"We should have seen this coming, instead of letting the limelight get to us." I paused and glanced up at my team. "*I* should have known better."

"You can't take this all on yourself, Chief," Chuck said with a look of concern. "We were all just as willing to play this game as anyone."

"He's right," agreed Felicia. "This isn't on you, Chief."

I stood back up and wiped the dust off my hands. They were a good team. Unfortunately, they were off base on this one.

"I appreciate your positions, but I'm in charge and therefore this is my responsibility."

"We're not children," Jasmine admonished. "You can no more force us to do anything than you can stop us if we really want to do something. We're in this together, Ian."

They were all nodding in agreement.

Technically, they were correct in what they were saying, but if I had spoken up earlier, they would have followed my lead. This could have been stopped right away, but we let the limelight affect our judgment. Any one of us had to know that this couldn't end well in the long run. That was abundantly clear the moment the abominable snowman launched that college kid with a backhand. Promotional stunts don't go out of their way to injure people. But there was no point in debating with my crew at the moment. Their sentiment was enough to demonstrate how they felt over what had happened. Regardless, the responsibility *was* mine.

"We obviously have a pixie on the loose," I stressed, "and the damn thing has to be stopped."

These were words you never expected to say as it related to pixies. Their kind was mostly just loudmouthed, vulgar, and irritating. They *could* fight, of course, but it didn't happen very often. And terrorizing a town? Never.

Serena touched my arm as she walked past to study the area where the bodies were. I felt a jolt of healing energy from her. She was trying to lift my emotions.

It helped a little.

"What are we looking for?" I asked the rest of the team.

"A pixie with incredibly powerful skill," mused Griff.

"Obviously," Jasmine spat and then frantically shook her hands. "I'm sorry, Griff. I'm just…" She looked away.

He didn't seem to take offense.

"In all of my years," Griff continued, "I have never heard of a pixie who was capable of encasing a normal in such fashion." He was wringing his fingers together as he watched Serena checking the area. "Not movable encasements, I mean. They could certainly imprison a person in something static, such as a wall. But these manifested creatures were mobile."

"What are you saying?" asked Felicia.

"I'm saying that we have something new here," he answered as if that were abundantly clear.

It was.

"It's worse than you guys think," announced Jasmine as Rachel returned. "They weren't merely encased. They *were* the creatures."

Rachel spoke up first. "What?"

"The damage to their skin," Serena explained while tilting one of the girls' head to the side, "the burning of their flesh, and the fact that there is dust literally pouring from their ears, eyes, mouths, and…well, likely everywhere, tells me that these people were completely engulfed by the pixie dust."

That was sobering.

"This should not be possible," Griff remarked in a hoarse voice. "The level of magic to infuse a normal is quite literally off the charts. But to convert one into a creature of that size and then control it?"

He didn't bother to answer his own question.

"We definitely have an uber pixie here, then," I breathed, trying to keep my anger under control. "I need to get back to base."

"Why?" asked Rachel.

"Because my last meeting with the Directors told me that they know more about these ubers than they're letting on."

Portman's white vans pulled up a moment later.

"Work with Portman and get this cleaned up, please," I instructed Griff and Chuck before I stormed off toward my car with Rachel in tow. "I'm going to try and get us some goddamn information!"

# CHAPTER 11

*I* was not in the mood to play around today. The Directors, who were my bosses, knew what was going on with these ubers and it was time I was let in on it. They sat in various places around the country, connecting in through some magic portal. It was like video conferencing but without monitors.

O was the head of the Vegas Crimson Focus Mages, Zack led up the Vegas Wolfpack, Silver ran the Vegas Vampire Coalition, and EQK was in charge of the Vegas Pixies. Typically these meetings were based around me watching them bicker with each other, but things had grown slightly more serious as of late.

"Mr. Dex," started O, "we are very sorry—"

"Are you?" I interrupted. "Seriously? Because it's sure as hell hard to tell."

I was fuming and they were silent. Usually they gave me a fair bit of backlash when I raised my voice at them. Tonight, I honestly didn't care.

"I've got five dead normals out there because of some

JOHN P. LOGSDON & CHRISTOPHER P. YOUNG

uber fucking pixie who has somehow figured out a way to morph people into monsters."

"What?" asked EQK.

"You heard me," I replied, looking in his direction. "One of your fellow pixies has learned how to turn normals into beasts. We just killed five of them."

"Fuck," he replied with a hiss.

"So your pixies aren't the upstanding citizens you always claim them to be, eh EQK?" Silver said, pushing buttons. "And here I thought they were above reproach."

I saw a wisp of EQK as he jumped up on the table and yelled, "Shove it up your ass, fang boy."

"Okay, okay," Zack chimed in, always the peacemaker. "There is no point in our fighting amongst ourselves. We clearly have a very important issue to get a handle on here."

"Yes," I agreed emphatically, "you do. And you can start by telling me what the hell you know about these ubers who have been turning up lately."

They were silent.

"Hello?" I pressed. "Don't go quiet on me now, guys. I have a crew out there that is beside themselves over what just happened. My job is to give them the information they need to be effective cops. Your job is to do the same for me."

"Mr. Dex," said O in a calm voice that made me want to leap through the mist and punch his lights out, "we are not always at liberty to provide you with information. Some things are classified for a reason."

"Classified, eh?" I mused, staring in his direction. I couldn't actually see him, but I knew where he was seated. "At least now I'm certain that you *do* know about these things."

There was no answer.

In all my years in dealing with the Directors, it was typically me sitting there while listening to them gripe at each other and act like a bunch of school children. Now that I needed something heavy, I was the primary one doing the talking.

But yelling at them wasn't going to solve anything.

"Look," I said, trying like mad to maintain my composure, "I don't know if any of you have ever walked the beat or not, but it's not easy out there. We're always under attack, we never know when trouble is coming, and we're almost always given far too little information to effectively do our jobs." I let that sink in before continuing. "People are dying out there, and this time it was by *our* hands. That includes you four."

"Fuck that, dick vein," EQK blurted in response. "We weren't anywhere near the incident when you assholes started blowing holes in shit. I swear to the great pixie that you idiots will kill just about anything."

"Don't forget that it was a pixie causing all of this mayhem, my tiny friend," Silver mocked.

"I'll kick your bloodless ass, if you don't shut your trap, Silver."

"Enough!" This time it was me yelling. Surprisingly, they quieted and nobody reprimanded me.

I counted slowly down from ten.

"The bottom line, gentlemen," I replied in a very slow, methodical voice, "is that I require more information than you're providing me. I cannot continue putting my crew in situations without knowing what I'm dealing with. It is unfair to them, to me, and to the people we are sworn to protect."

O leaned forward, giving me just enough of a glimpse of his face to try and commit it to memory. No luck. The visual dissipated like smoke in front of a high-speed fan. It was so aggravating.

"Ian," he said, going completely informal, "there are many

things that we cannot tell you, and I know that's difficult for you to deal with, but you must understand that we have our reasons."

"O is right," Zack stated. "We can no more share every nuance with you than you can run out to the normal community and let them in on the fact that supernaturals exist."

"Agreed," Silver said a moment later.

I wanted to jump up and yell at them. I wanted to call them all a bunch of bastards. But what would that accomplish? I'd feel better for a few minutes, sure, but it wouldn't get them on my side any more than they already were. They weren't going to spill the beans, that was for certain.

So I put up my hands, stood up, and walked out, not saying a word as I left them there to stew in their silence.

As soon as I entered my office I found Rachel sitting on the opposite side of my desk, waiting for me.

I plopped down in my chair, feeling defeated.

What was the point of the Directors anyway? It didn't seem like they did much to help me. They were great at grilling me for information and acting all uppity and powerful, but where the hell were they when I needed them? Hiding behind their secrets, that's where.

I glanced up at Rachel, and that's when I noticed a mug of something on my desk.

There was steam coming off the top.

"What's that?" I asked, confused.

She shifted slightly. "Tea."

"Tea?"

She nodded.

I leaned forward and looked inside the cup. Sure enough, it was tea.

Now, don't get me wrong. I'm actually quite a fan of tea,

especially when my stress level was through the roof, much like it was right now. But Rachel had never brought me…

I looked up.

"What's going on?" I asked dubiously.

*"She's serving us, you dope,"* noted The Admiral. *"Nice, right?"*

*"Honestly, shut up."*

"Nothing," she said, standing up and walking around.

"Rachel," I whispered the moment she started straightening up my desk, "have you been drinking?"

She stopped. "What?"

"You've brought me tea and you're cleaning my desk." My eyes went wide and my heart nearly stopped. "Oh shit, you're not pregnant, are you?"

"No!" Her yell started my heart beating again. "What the hell, Ian?"

"I'm just…" I squinted. "What's going on?"

"I'm trying to be more supportive," she said in a huff. "Is that okay or are you going to yell at me about that, too?"

"Oh," I said, staring down at the tea. "I…wow." I glanced up. "Thanks, babe."

She softened at that.

"You're welcome."

I took a sip. It was good. Chamomile. Relaxing.

"I don't suppose the Directors were any help?" she asked, resuming her seat.

"Are they ever?"

"Not very often," she replied. "At least not from what you've told us."

They *had* supported me when Rachel was kidnapped in London. Other than that, it was rare to get useful intel out of them. Still, I suppose it wasn't easy being in their positions, especially when it came to working with someone like EQK.

"I think it's time to pull the team together," I said, pushing myself up from the desk. "We need to figure out how to approach this pixie problem we have."

# CHAPTER 12

*M*y crew was deadly serious when I walked into the room. We were usually a bit more lighthearted than this, even though our work wasn't exactly all pixies and fairy dust.

Okay, bad example.

The point was that things had gotten pretty heated. We needed to get loose again or we were going to start making mistakes. There's a saying in hockey that if you go on a losing streak you'll start holding your stick too tight and that'll make you miss easy shots. Frankly, I never had a problem with holding my stick too tight. In fact, I rather preferred it that way.

"All right, everyone," I called out, bringing their focus on me, "we all know the score and we're all pretty pissed off about it. But getting more and more angry isn't going to help us solve anything. So let's table our emotions as much as possible and get back to work." I scanned the area. "Where's Turbo?"

"I'm here," he said, zipping into the room a moment later. "Sorry, I was trying to find my cap."

"Good to see you have your priorities in place."

"Thanks, Chief."

I frowned at him.

"Right, so we have a pixie running around town creating monsters out of normals. Any suggestions on how we can track the little asshole?" I then caught myself. "Sorry, Turbo."

He looked up at me. "About what?"

"Uh...never mind." I coughed. Then I looked at him again. "You don't happen to know of any pixies who are *really* good with their dust, do you?"

Turbo turned and put his hands on his hips, giving me a stern look.

"No," he said flatly.

"What's with the attitude? I just asked a question."

"You asked it as if I know every pixie in the world. Just because I'm a pixie doesn't mean I know *all* of them." He sniffed at me while shaking his head. "Do you know every amalgamite in the world?"

"Yes," I replied without hesitation.

"Okay, bad example," he acquiesced. "Still, I—"

"He was just asking a question, Turbo," Chuck said, coming to my defense. "There's no reason to get all wound up about it."

Turbo crossed his arms and harrumphed. Then he groaned and said, "Okay, okay, I'm sorry. It's just that whenever someone in my race does something like this, everyone starts giving me the stink-eye."

"Everyone?" I asked. "Like who?"

"Nobody here," he replied. "But people in my apartment complex shake their heads at me and such, and I don't even want to talk about what people say to me when I go to Starbucks for my morning coffee. It's annoying."

Before you ask, some Starbucks—and most every store

out there—have hidden areas set aside for supers who aren't able to shape change.

"That's not cool," said Felicia. "Is this happening already? This pixie situation just started."

"It not happening yet, no," Turbo admitted. "I just know it's coming and so I'm touchy about it."

It was kind of tough for me to empathize seeing that there was only one of me, but I could surmise the feeling. My guess was it was similar to what I felt whenever I took my clothes off around a new chick. They always assumed I was a Chippendales dancer.

"Well, look," I said gently, "if you can figure out a way for us to track this dude, it'll take him out of the public eye quicker."

Serena sat up suddenly, her eyes darting around.

"I think I can track him if I can get to wherever he is as soon as he's cast his dust," she said. "I'd have to be there within ten minutes or so, though. After that, the connection would fade and I'd miss my window."

"Hmmm," said Turbo as he began pacing around on the table. Then he snapped his fingers and pointed at Serena. "I can rig up the cameras we have around town to track any anomalies. If anything hits, I can have the system send you all screen captures and locations. You'd be able to drive around town and pick up anything that happens in a heartbeat."

"That's good," I said, nodding. "I could probably get a permit for an instant portal for you, too, Serena. Considering the circumstances, that should be doable."

I'd have Lydia get in contact with the Netherworld Portal Authority and get the proper permissions. It wasn't always allowed, but this was an extreme case. Plus, if push came to shove, I had a feeling that the Directors would step in at this point to make it happen.

They owed me one.

Hell, they owed *all* of us one.

"That's great. How long will it take you to get the tracking set up, Turbo?"

He scratched his chin.

"That depends on how fancy you want it," he answered. "I can make it in color, if that would help. Oooh, I could add a three-dimensional effect, with—"

I held up my hands to stop him. "We just need it to notify us when the dude casts his spell, Turbo."

"Well, in that case…" He started doing calculations in the air, squinting his left eye a few times in the process. Finally, he nodded to himself and said, "Three weeks."

I put my hands on the table and leaned forward until I was right in his face, giving him a dark stare.

"You'll have it done by tomorrow night, Turbo," I instructed in a cold voice. "I don't care what resources you need, and I don't care if you have to work straight through until it's done. You're going to make it happen. Are we clear?"

He nodded and I backed away.

"Jeez," he mumbled a few seconds later. "Why bother to ask how much time I need if you're just going to yell at me about it anyway?"

I rolled my eyes and looked over at Serena.

"Anything you need to do in order to get your tracking plan underway?"

She nodded, glancing over at Turbo. "Yeah, but don't worry, I'll have it done by tomorrow night."

I sighed.

# CHAPTER 13

$S$ince I had two crew members working around the clock, I stayed at the office as well. I wasn't the type of manager who demanded that others do something I wasn't willing to do myself.

Rachel had gone back to my place to get some sleep, giving me much needed time to go over documents and such.

Each of my officers were on their five-year review cycle. That meant I had to write up their positives and negatives, ride with them for a week each, and give them deserved increases in pay, etc. Overworld PPD officers tended to get the majority of their expenses handled because they were on the clock a lot. Still, if you wanted an upgraded place to live, that came out of your own pocket. This wasn't an issue for me because I was independently wealthy, but that wasn't the case for everyone on my crew.

*"Puddin',"* Lydia said through the connector, *"I've got Paula Rose on the phone for you."*

I stared at the mountain of files that Rachel had tidied up for me and blew out a long breath.

*"Put her through to my normal line, Lydia."* My cell beeped,

signaling that the connection was set. I put her on speaker. "Hi, Paula."

"Do you have any suggestions for how I'm supposed to handle this, Ian?"

She was talking about the dead normals, of course, and she knew damn well that I had no answers for her. It wasn't my job to put the spin on things. If it was, I wouldn't be staring at all of these files right now.

"Sorry, Paula. I don't know what to tell you."

"They're going to have my head on a platter," she moaned. "This isn't going to be one of those things that easily disappears, and I don't think anyone is going to go for a new show where supernatural cops kill touristing normals."

"Probably not," I agreed. "You *do* realize that we didn't know there were people in those dinosaurs, I hope?"

"Obviously," she replied. "I suppose I could just say that it was all due to technical difficulties. That would solve it after some time, anyway."

"Doesn't help their families," I pointed out.

Neither of us said anything for a little time. Paula clearly felt just as bad regarding what had happened as I did. She was a corporate mogul in the making, sure, but she wasn't so powerful that she'd lost her conscience...and hopefully she never would be.

"So you're dating Rachel again?" she asked out of the blue. "I know that was an awkward change of topics, but there's really not much more we can say about the other situation."

Ah ha. That was the *real* reason for her call.

"Yes, we're dating again."

"I have to say that she was kind of nice to me and Murphy earlier." She paused. "Well, not at first. Actually, she was pretty rude at first, but once she apologized and everything, she was almost pleasant to work with."

I looked up at the ceiling, putting my head in my hands.

"I'm glad to hear it. I think she's really trying to make things work this time."

"And you?"

"Me?"

"Do *you* want things to work out, Ian?"

"Yeah," I said sincerely. "I really think I do. It's not going to be easy, and I'm sure there will be some bumps along the way, but it's pretty obvious that Rachel and I were meant for each other." That's when my subconscious reminded me that Paula was one of my ex-girlfriends. "Uh, I, uh—"

She laughed.

"Don't worry, Ian. You didn't hurt my feelings. You and I never would have made it beyond the physical. We both know that."

"True."

Paula and I had been *very* compatible in the bedroom, but we couldn't function in normal society very well. Both of us were career-driven, and those careers were of the type where I made her life difficult by putting her in situations like the one we were in right now. That, in turn, bled into our physical relationship, knocking us out of sync repeatedly.

*"I'd still love to go for a swim in her canal,"* noted The Admiral out of nowhere.

*"Under normal circumstances,"* I agreed, *"so would I."*

*"What's normal? She's a chick, right? You and I are a team. You sweet talk 'em and I make them call us 'God.'"*

"Classy."

"Anyway," I spoke up before The Admiral could fire another verbal volley my way, "I'm sure we've not seen the last of the pixie who is messing with us, but you can rest assured that we're going to be exceedingly cautious before we just blow away anything he or she creates."

"Do you have any leads?"

"Not yet," I answered. "Turbo is in the process of putting

together a way to detect whenever the pixie creates the beasts. He should be done by tomorrow night. Serena is testing ways to track the guy from the scene, assuming she can get there quickly enough."

"Good." Paula sounded very tired. "I *do* think that a show like this would be very profitable."

"Yeah."

"Maybe we can plan for it to happen in a few years, after everything blows over."

"Maybe, yeah." I drummed my fingers on the desk. "Well, I'd better get rolling, Paula. I have a lot of paperwork to do and I can't ever seem to find the time to do it."

We said our goodbyes and I pulled the first folder over and began to study it.

Officer Chuck Taylor. He'd been on the squad for twenty-three years. Vampire. Good with weapons and hand-to-hand combat. Fast thinker. Loyal. These were all things I knew, but the forms were to remind me of each positive point so I wouldn't have to drum up things on my own. Seemed silly. Maybe bigger precincts, like the one in London, would require this little bundle of reminders, but when you worked as closely with your crew as I did, you were constantly reminded of their individual strengths and weaknesses.

Still, it was kind of nice to have it all wrapped up in a document.

The basics, anyway.

Forms couldn't easily collate the nuances. That was for me to manage either by myself or through discussions with fellow officers.

The other officers weren't likely to be overly critical, though. This was mostly because they also wanted a raise and they knew that Chuck would be giving them a recommendation just as they were recommending him. You scratch my back, I scratch yours. You stab my back, I *severely* scratch yours.

But so what? My crew were all friends. Hell, I'd go as far as to say they were family. The only family I'd ever really had. They would no more give each other a bad reference than I would.

Thinking of them in that light made me smile.

Maybe doing these reviews wasn't going to be that difficult after all.

# CHAPTER 14

*T*he valkyries were all standing before me in the arena on the seventh level of Hell. They were almost completely naked, except for their tall, silver boots.

*Why this place was ever considered "Hell" was beyond me.*

*"We've been waiting for you, Ian," said the valkyrie known as Valerie. "It is lonely down here, you know?"*

*"Sorry, ladies," I said, but the voice didn't quite belong to me. I mean, it was my voice, but the inflection was off. "I've been dealing with some personal issues. Mostly with me being a pussy and such. But now that you all are around to ride me into oblivion, I think things will start to turn around."*

"Ian, sweetie?" said Lydia, jolting me from my dream.

"Huh?"

I was hunched over my desk with my head on Turbo's file. Obviously I'd fallen asleep, and it was clear that The Admiral was doing everything he could to get my mind off Rachel, which was why the voice in my dream sounded so familiar. I wanted to slap him, to be honest, but that would have only proved to make things worse.

*"I won't tell, if you won't,"* announced The Admiral.

I groaned and rubbed my eyes, waiting for my brain to become fully awake.

Then I snagged a tissue and sopped up the puddle of drool I'd left on Turbo's file.

Ew.

"*What's up, Lydia?*"

"*We just got word that—*"

"Chief," yelled Turbo as he zipped into the room, "my scanners are working! They just picked up massive werewolves down at the Flamingo."

"Shit," I said, trying to get my brain up to full power while rubbing my neck. "What time is it?"

"Almost six," he said.

"At night?"

"Yeah," Turbo said slowly. "You okay, Chief?" Then he buzzed over and pointed at the open file on my desk. "Hey, is that about my review? And why is it wet?"

"Never mind that," I answered, slamming the file shut. "Is Serena on the way to the Flamingo already?"

"She left almost immediately, using the direct portal."

"Perfect," I said, silently thanking Lydia for getting authorization for that. I then yelled out to the room, "Lydia, please get the other officers down to the Flamingo and let them know I'll be there in a few minutes."

"I'm coming with you," announced Turbo.

"You sure?"

"Yeah. I might be able to help."

I wasn't about to argue the point with him. He may not know every pixie in the world, which made sense when I really thought about it, but he knew better than I did how they ticked. If nothing else, he might be able to help us bring this to a resolution more quickly.

We bolted out the door and nearly got to my Aston Martin when I heard Warren yell, "Hey, Chief, wait up!"

I hadn't seen Warren all that much since the incident with Charlotte the dragon. He had taken that entire ordeal pretty hard. I can't say that I blamed him, but it honestly wasn't his fault. Charlotte had used her wiles on him and she'd fooled all of us.

"What's up, Warren?" I asked.

"I've been working all day on a spell that will help everyone know if there are normals encased in the creatures. If there are, I have another spell to protect them while allowing you to destroy the beasts around them." He ran his fingers through this long scraggly beard. "Well, it *should* anyway. I haven't had much time to test it."

It was better than nothing.

"Okay, come on, then."

"Shotgun!" called Turbo, signaling that he wanted to sit up front.

We poured into the Aston Martin and I revved the engine.

While it looked ridiculous, Turbo insisted that he be belted in. So I ran the seatbelt across and locked it. Then he flew up to the midpoint of the seat and climbed under the belt.

I shook my head and started driving.

*"Everyone on their way?"* I asked through my connector.

A bunch of tired affirmatives came back.

*"Good. Nobody engage those things until we get there."* I checked the rearview mirror and noticed that Warren appeared apprehensive. I decided to give him some public kudos. *"Also, note that Warren has been doing research on a way for us to detect and protect any normals that may be encased in these things, so we'll have that going for us."*

*"Nice,"* said Jasmine.

*"Thanks, Warren,"* agreed Chuck.

*"Well done,"* stated Griff.

Warren's face was on the mend.

That was good.

"*All right, everyone,*" I said, feeling that our feel-good moment was complete, "*no theatrics this time. We go in and take care of business.*"

"*Shall I notify The Spin, lover?*" asked Lydia.

"*Yeah, baby,*" I replied, giving her a little bit of flirt back, which I made sure to do now and then in order to keep her purring. "*Also, tell the cops and security crews at the Flamingo to clear the area. We don't want crowds this time, if we can help it.*"

"*You got it, sweet tushy.*"

"*Ugh,*" said Rachel.

"*Brother,*" The Admiral piped up, "*it sure would be great if we could get Lydia put into the body of an android or something, wouldn't it?*"

"*Yeah,*" I said after a few moments, "*I'll give you that one.*"

"*It wouldn't be cheating either, right? I mean, she'd be like a big vibrator. Vibrators are cool, right? Rachel has one and we don't get all up in her face when she's using it. Actually, I guess we do sometimes, but not in a complaining way, if you see what I mean.*"

I merely shook my head in response. Why did I have to have a dick that talked to me?

We zoomed down the road until we got to the Flamingo.

"Uh, Chief," said Turbo, straining under the pressure of the belt against his chest, "that looks like one massive crowd."

I groaned.

"*Ian,*" Rachel croaked through the connector, "*we have injuries here. The wolves are snapping at people.*"

"Shit. Lydia—"

"*Already have Portman on the way, dear. Please be careful, love muffin.*"

"We *will!*" spat Rachel.

# CHAPTER 15

*I* jumped out of the Aston Martin and took off toward the front entrance. There were a few bodies down, but it didn't look like anyone was dead. Dying? Possibly. But not dead.

"Warren," I hollered as the lanky wizard caught up to me, panting like mad, "cast your spell on these wolves, quick."

"Okay," he said, heaving. "One…sec…"

Honestly, if a person on my squad couldn't run a couple hundred feet without passing out, they needed to start an exercise program. This wasn't some damn high school gym class, after all.

"Dude," yelled out a drunk guy who looked to be in his late twenties as he ran up to one of the wolves, "bite my arm!"

The wolf obliged.

The guy screamed.

"Get him out of there," I yelled at the security guard who was nearest him. Then I turned toward the crowd. "Everyone, listen to me. This is *not* a joke. These things are dangerous. The next person who steps out of line is going to be sent to jail. Are we clear?"

They booed me.

I have to say that it didn't feel nearly as good as it felt being cheered.

"Sorry," Warren said as he slowly caught his breath. "Okay, I'm ready."

With a flick of his wand and some type of incantation that I couldn't understand, though he sounded hilarious when he said it, a haze fell over the wolves.

"They're clean," he said a moment later.

"What's that mean?" I asked.

"No humans are inside of them. They're just shells."

I gave him a hard stare. "You're *absolutely* sure about that, Warren?"

He swallowed, took a deep breath, and then nodded.

"Okay," I said to my crew. "You heard the man. Let's light these fuckers up."

"Wait!" Serena stopped us. "I'm very close to finding a scent for the pixie who is doing this. I just need another…" She trailed off for a second. She was using some device against the wall that was behind the wolves. "Got him."

"Got him?" Chuck asked. "What do you mean?"

"The uber pixie," she explained. "I have his trail. I can track him."

As if our pal the pixie had just heard Serena's claim, a flash of light shot down from the top of the Flamingo roof, striking the wolves. They all howled so loudly that I thought certain my ears were going to split.

The crowd covered their ears, wincing.

"Kill those fucking things," I commanded, whipping out Boomy and firing round after round at them. "Now!"

My mages started with the glowing-hands thing, but the

wolves weren't like the past pixie creations. These apparently had been given the ability to roam.

And roam they did.

Right into the Flamingo.

"After them," I said, taking the lead and running after the damn beasts. "Serena, take Turbo and Warren and stay on the pixie's trail."

"On it," she said.

I could only hope Warren would be able to keep up with her. Good thing I knew Serena well enough to understand that she wouldn't lose track of the pixie just to make sure that Warren kept pace with her.

Priorities.

We hit the casino floor, chasing the wolves with all we had. The damn things were fast, though.

"Going into wolf form," Felicia announced as she kept running.

The transition was pretty incredible to watch. She ran faster and faster and then leaped through the air, switching from human to wolf while flying in a large arc until she landed on all fours.

She jumped again, crashing into the back of one of the three pixie wolves we were chasing. While the thing was made of dust, that just made it easier for Felicia to tear a hole through its neck. It also gave Rachel, Griff, and Jasmine enough time to launch a stream of flames at the fallen wolf as Felicia rolled and took off toward the next in the batch.

"Griff and Chuck," I said as I kept running, "finish that one up and then follow us. Rachel and Jasmine, come on!"

The dogs bolted toward the east entrance. While I was no wolf, I had elements of wolf in me. That gave me speed and strength, so I was having a decent time of keeping up with them, but Rachel and Jasmine were lagging farther and farther behind.

I got to the entrance and saw the two wolves facing in. They were staring down Felicia, who had taken to stalking forward like she was getting ready to pounce.

"*Felicia,*" I called through the connector. She hesitated. "*You can't take on two of them.*"

There was no response to that, but I could sense she disagreed with me.

"*There is no point in you getting killed. Wait for backup.*"

She growled.

Suddenly, one of the pixie wolves barked at the other. In response, the second wolf barked back and then sped out of the casino. I went to take off after it, but his pal lunged at me.

Fortunately for me, Felicia intercepted his attack, knocking him off-path as I continued after the wolf that had left the scene.

"*Jasmine,*" I said, "*flame that damn wolf that Felicia is fighting as soon as you can. Chuck—*"

"*We've already destroyed the first wolf, Chief,*" he replied before I could say anything more. "*And we'll be at the east entrance in fifteen seconds to kill the second one.*"

"*Good. Rachel, get your ass in gear!*"

"*I'm coming! I'm coming!*"

"*Okay,*" The Admiral stated, nearly causing me to lose my footing, "*I do have to say that I rather like it when Rachel yells that particular phrase.*"

Unbelievable.

# CHAPTER 16

*T*he wolf ran like the wind, not tiring in the least. I, on the other hand, was starting to wheeze like Warren after he climbed a small flight of stairs. If it weren't for the fact that my body healed so quickly, the burning in my legs would have locked me up faster than a succubus at a nudie bar.

*"Now you're talkin'."*

Everyone would be able to track me without a problem, so I just kept churning my legs. The connector system allowed us to know where each PPD officer was at all times, unless we turned off the tracking system for personal reasons, or, like in the case of when Rachel had been kidnapped, if the signal got cut off. We typically didn't employ this system unless we needed to, though, because it took some effort to engage. It wasn't like I could just say, "Track Rachel" and my legs would just start running in that direction. Though, that would be cool. Then again, my legs would probably force me to take off across a busy intersection and that would make for a bad day.

The wolf turned a corner and something told me to slow down.

I listened.

*"We're on our way, Chief,"* Chuck said through the connector. *"Two puppies down."*

*"I'd prefer you not use that terminology,"* Felicia admonished. Obviously, she'd returned to her human form. *"So unless you'd like me to start referring to vampires as itty bitty bats, I suggest you not do that."*

*"You're right,"* Chuck said. *"Sorry."*

I creeped up to the corner of the building where the pixie wolf had turned and peered around the edge.

*"Yikes,"* I said, fighting to keep my cool. *"Guys, there are ten wolves here."*

*"Ten?"* said Jasmine.

*"Yeah, and I don't know if any of them are normals or not."*

*"Where are you, Chief?"* asked Warren.

*"Track me,"* I replied.

*"Oh, right."* A couple of seconds later, he said, *"You're not far from us at all. I can be there in about thirty seconds, if I run."*

*"Make it a minute and walk,"* I stated. *"Won't do us any good if you're out of breath."*

*"I'll be on the other side of the building from you."*

*"Doesn't matter,"* I replied as Rachel approached. *"We just need you to do your stuff so we know what we're dealing with."*

*"And so you can protect any normals that may be encased in those things,"* Rachel added.

*"Right."*

By the time the rest of my crew arrived, I saw a fog falling over the heads of the wolves who were stoically waiting to destroy us. They didn't seem bothered by this magical invasion, and since Serena was hot on the trail of the uber pixie who created them, I wasn't so worried that he'd cast some naughty spell on them.

"*No normals,*" Warren said. "*You're all clear.*"

"*Thanks, Warren. Get back to Serena and help her find that damn pixie.*"

"*She's already found him,*" Warren replied.

"*Oh?*"

"*I have,*" Serena interrupted, whispering. "*He's moving slowly at this point. I don't know if he's tired or simply not worried that we'll catch up to him, but he's taking his time.*"

That was probably because he assumed his pack of wolves were going to make minced meat out of us. Another glance around the corner made me concede the possibility.

"Can't we just sneak around the other way?" suggested Rachel aloud.

"You mean attack them from the rear?"

"No, Ian, I mean bypass them completely and just get after the pixie."

I gave her an appraising look.

"Actually, that's a great—"

"Uh…" she said, pointing. "Never mind."

I turned and saw the drooling jaw of a wolf peeking around the corner at me. Then another stepped up beside that one. And another, and another, and…well, you get the idea.

It seemed they'd become impatient with waiting on us.

Now, one or two wolves wouldn't be so bad to deal with in a situation like this, but ten was a little much, at least without a proper plan.

But my years of leading this team told me there was always one tactic that stood the test of time. It had saved us from the brink of ruin on more occasions than I could recall. In fact, it was probably the single most important strategy we had ever employed.

"Run!"

We took off back the way we came, but cut to the left at

the other side of the building we were hugging so we could catch up to Serena.

There was no way we were going to be able to outrun these things. I could make a show of it, as could Felicia if she turned again, but everyone else would get caught eventually.

"Drop some flames or something," I cried while firing Boomy over my shoulder. "Chuck and Felicia, shoot at the damn things to slow them down."

Griff started launching fireballs backwards without even looking. Of all the people on my crew, he was the oldest. He was still in far better shape than Warren, but his pace was slowing enough to demonstrate his age. Of course, with age comes experience. As a testament to that fact, Griff's fireballs were accurately striking targets left and right. Best of all, they were hitting legs.

"Fire at their legs, Charles," he called to his partner.

Chuck did and the beasts wailed in response.

That would give us some more time while they had to repair and rebuild themselves.

"I have an idea," Rachel said. "Jasmine and Griff, just throw a sea of flame at the ground. All you've got."

A wolf was within striking range of Jasmine, but Felicia shot its front paw off, causing it to bellow in rage.

Rachel yelled, "Everyone, jump!"

We didn't have to be told twice.

A split-second later, the ground directly under us and them turned into fire. We all cleared it upon landing, but the wolves weren't so lucky. Only one of them had been in mid-flight when the spell got launched.

It crashed into Griff and ripped into his side.

The rest of the wolves stopped instantly as their legs turned to glass. Jasmine and Rachel flamed the rest of their bodies as Felicia and I commenced blowing them to bits.

Chuck went after the wolf who was attacking his partner.

Honestly, that wolf didn't have a chance. Chuck was so incensed that he lifted the thing off the ground and carried it to the pool of fire. It was clawing and chomping at him the entire time, but hate was on Chuck's side. He dumped it into the fire and then shattered it with three perfectly placed shots.

Griff was groaning and blood was pooling around him.

His eyes rolled up into his head.

# CHAPTER 17

*R*achel and Jasmine began channeling energy into Griff, doing what they could to keep him alive. Mages were notoriously resilient, but they weren't dead-proof.

"Come on, Griff," Chuck said with desperation in his voice, "you gotta hang on, man."

One thing was for sure, I was going to fuck that pixie up, once I got hold of his tiny-winged ass, anyway.

*"Lydia,"* I called to base, *"I need you to get a portal authorization right now. Let the hospital know that we have an officer down."*

*"On it,"* she replied, keeping her response business-like this time. Not even thirty seconds went by before she said, *"Authorization is complete for both Officers Benchley and Taylor. Code is 1-3-8-8-7."*

*"And the hospital?"*

*"They've been notified and have a team rushing to the null ward."*

*"Thank you, Lydia."* I knelt beside Chuck and put my arm on his shoulder. "Hey, buddy, you both have immediate

portal authorization." I gave him the code. "Doctors are waiting. Go, now. We'll manage the pixie."

He looked up at me with fury in his eyes. "Make him pay, Ian."

"Don't worry about that," I replied. "Take care of Griff."

They blinked from view, leaving just the remnants of blood from where Griff had been lying. Rachel, Jasmine, and Felicia were doing their best to keep the tears at bay. As I said, we were like family.

"Serena, Turbo, and Warren," I announced while starting to run purposefully toward her location, "Griff has been sent back to the hospital with serious injuries. Chuck went with him."

"Damn it," Serena hissed.

"Is he going to be okay?" asked Warren.

"I hope so," I answered. "He looked pretty rough. Right now, though, we need to focus on making sure that pixie doesn't do any more damage than he already has."

"Agreed," said Turbo. "This guy is a blight on my community, and if you have met any pixies, you'll know that's really saying something."

After spending over five years dealing with the constant barrage of insults from EQK, I found that difficult to argue. Not all pixies were like him, obviously—a case in point being Turbo— but most were.

"Tell me you're still on the guy's tail," I said as we neared Serena's position. "We see you guys."

They turned toward us and then pointed up ahead. The pixie was flying merrily along, no doubt unaware that he had us on his trail. That was perfect.

Felicia must have thought so, too, because she had her Desert Eagle out and was aiming it right at the little fucker's back.

I put my hand on her arm to stop her.

"We can't afford a missed shot, Felicia," I said gently, "and even if you're on target, we don't know if he'll have a shield up. He looks to be exceedingly confident, but I doubt he's stupid."

She sighed irritably, but nodded and stuck her Eagle back in its holster.

"Let's just stay on his tail until he gets back to whatever he's using as a lair."

I started moving quickly enough to keep the pixie in sight, but not so fast that we'd be noticed.

Serena was by my side, looking down at a device she was holding. It looked like some kind of instrument you'd see in *Star Trek*.

"What's that do?"

"Hmmm?" she murmured and then glanced over at me. "Oh, it's keeping track of his energy signature. Kind of like what we do with our connectors, but since we don't have one for him, I'm using this. I had to first get his signature on it, which was why I needed to get to the scene immediately after he set up his last creation."

"But we can see him just fine now," I noted.

"Until we can't." She kept her eyes on the unit. "As you said, he's probably heading to his lair. I doubt that it'll be visible to us."

"Good point."

Suddenly, the pixie stopped.

I motioned everyone to get back against the building we were standing beside. We pressed against the bricks just as our prey spun around and started studying the area. He flew back toward our position a little bit, but not close enough that he could have easily spotted us.

"Do you—" started Warren with a whisper.

"*Shhh*," I growled through the connector. "*What the fuck, dude?*"

Warren clamped his mouth shut and hung his head slightly.

"*Sorry*," he said, this time using the connector.

The pixie spun again and continued along, but this time he was moving quicker. Either he knew we were on to him or he just had one of those feelings like he was being watched. I doubted he'd heard Warren speaking.

"*Let's go*," I said, pushing off the wall and moving to a full jog after the little turd. "*Stick as close to the walls as possible, and no talking unless it's through the connector.*"

Nobody said a word. We just kept pace through the streets, hugging the shadows wherever possible. I couldn't see the little prick anymore, but Serena was tracking him without a problem.

"Stop," Warren yelped aloud and then quickly covered his mouth.

We did and I shot him a look, nearly ready to stick my foot up his ass.

"Oh, shit," Rachel groaned. She'd said it out loud, too.

So much for keeping to the connector.

My wizard and two mages started frantically studying the area. Finally, they looked up at each other and then at me.

"What?" I implored.

"Notification rune," Warren squeaked.

"Uh…"

"He's coming back," Serena breathed, pointing at the tracker she was holding. "What do we do?"

I cracked my neck, took out Boomy, stuck in a fresh magazine, and then looked up into the night sky.

"We do what we're best at," I said without inflection. "We're going to kick his fucking ass."

## CHAPTER 18

*T*he uber pixie flew into view and looked down at us. Felicia didn't bother to hold back this time. She pointed and fired her Eagle. It deflected off a shield. The pixie *did* bounce away, but he flew right back, unaffected.

"You were right," she said, grunting. "I hate those fucking shields."

Jasmine and Rachel lit up their hands and cast spells at the little dude, but he just moved out of the way, expertly dodging each of their volleys like it was nothing.

He cackled at us and then turned and zipped down the street so fast that my eyes couldn't process the speed. Honestly, at the rate he was moving he could have burst right through any one of us like a bullet. That was a scary thought.

"He's quick," choked Turbo.

"Can you move like that?" I asked, reminding myself that *his* name was Turbo!

"No," he replied. "I've never seen any pixie move that fast, but I can say that when we turn on the jets, it tires us out quickly. He can't possibly maintain that for long."

"Don't forget he's an uber, though," Rachel noted. Then

she put up a finger. "He's got a shield, but what if we set a net for him?"

"What do you mean?"

"I cast a spell on the one side," she explained, "Jasmine hits the other, and we close in on him while you guys shoot at him, bouncing him around until he's sealed in tight."

I gave her a look. "You *just* noted how fast he was moving, right?"

"Yes, but Turbo also pointed out that he may not be able to do that forever." She held up a hand at me. "I know that he's an uber, but even Reese had to use demons to keep his power flowing at full. Logic dictates that this guy won't have an unlimited supply of mojo either." She turned and looked at the pixie off in the distance. "If we wear him down, he'll be trapped."

"What's he doing?" asked Felicia, stepping up.

"I was just wondering the same thing," Rachel said, continuing her stare at him. "If I were to guess, I'd say he's dumping a fair amount of pixie dust."

Serena held up the tracker. It was glowing like a goddamn Christmas tree.

I nodded at the device. "I'm guessing that's not good?"

"Your guess would be correct," she replied. "He's creating something."

"Then let's get the hell down there and stop him," I said, taking off at a full run. "Get your hands glowing, ladies. And, Warren, I don't care how out of breath you are when we get there, you'd better have your spell at the ready or we might end up killing humans again."

"I'll be ready, Chief," he replied stoically, though his breathing was already labored. "Just need to get close enough to cast the spell."

I direct-connected to him as we continued our run. *"Look, Warren, I don't want to seem insensitive to the fact that you're a wizard and wizards are notorious for not doing much but sitting around and studying. However, if you're going to be in the field with us, you've got to be in better shape than this."*

"You're right, Chief," he replied. The nice thing about using the connector instead of yelling back and forth was that you couldn't hear someone gasping with each word when they were exhausted. *"I think I'll create an elixir of stamina that I can bring along."*

*"Good idea."* We often had elixirs with us whenever we could prepare ahead of time. Some of the mages kept them on hand anyway. *"Remember that Serena is well-versed in creating all sorts of elixirs."*

Finally, we got near enough to the area to see that there was a small army of vampires waiting for us. I fired shot after shot at the uber pixie, bouncing him around until he finally gave me the finger and took off, leaving us to face our new foe.

There were only seven of them, but that would be enough to wreak havoc if we didn't act quickly.

"No screwing around this time," I yelled. "Burn their legs and we'll work our way up."

Rachel and Jasmine shot flames at their feet, but the vampires merely looked down at the flames, glanced back up, and smiled. I knew the damn things were made of dust, but they looked incredibly real.

I gulped. "Uh…what just happened?"

"The flames didn't work," said Turbo.

I frowned at him.

"Are you sure?" My voice was laced with sarcasm, but he didn't seem to notice. "Serena, any idea what we do now?"

"Run?"

We'd already employed that strategy once tonight. But it was still pretty high on my list at the moment. I didn't want another of my officers to get stuck in the hospital, after all.

That thought made me think of Griff.

I had to put that behind me, though. We needed to focus on the problem at hand.

"Try ice," I said.

Rachel launched a volley.

Nothing.

The vampires began laughing in the way vampires do. Arrogantly. There was some serious authenticity in that uber pixie's spell-casting.

Felicia took a step forward and shot one of them. This time it didn't even penetrate. It just ricocheted into the night.

"I'm really starting to hate this guy," I hissed. "Warren, are there normals in there or not?"

"Oh, damn," he said, shaking himself back to life. "I'm...damn. Sorry."

He quickly cast his spell and the vampires stared up at the fog as it descended on them. They didn't seem concerned. I couldn't say I would be either after having fireballs, ice barrages, and bullets essentially bounce away like they were nothing.

"No," he said, "but wait…"

He walked forward, moving closer and closer to the vampires like someone trying to see if there *really* was a spider in the corner or if it was just a piece of lint.

"*Warren?*" I said in warning.

He kept moving.

"*Warren?*" I singsonged it this time.

He still kept moving.

"Damn it, Warren," I yelled straight out, "those things are going to fucking kill you!"

He froze and turned back to us with an "Eureka!" expression lighting up his face.

"Energy pulses," he bellowed as the closest one reached out toward him. "Now!"

# CHAPTER 19

*W*arren hit the ground as Rachel and Jasmine shot energy through the air, swamping the pixie vampires in a bath of sparks. The world hummed as if we were standing next to a massive generator.

The vampires froze.

Their eyes began to glow blue as a white sheen covered their bodies.

"Get the hell out of there, Warren!" Rachel yelled.

Warren crawled as quickly as he could until he was just out of the electrical field. Then he got up and ran. If he did this kind of thing a few times a week, I daresay he may end up being in decent enough shape not to cough up a lung every time he exerted himself.

That said, it was evident that Rachel and Jasmine were starting to tire. The electricity flowing from their hands was losing its fervor slightly.

"What do we do?" I asked.

"We need to get more energy into them," Jasmine said. "We need Griff."

"That's not going to happen. Any other ideas?"

They both shook their heads.

It was a shame we weren't allowed to carry Empirics with us. A powerful little electrical grenade would be quite useful at the moment.

"Warren," I said, "can you help them?"

"Uh...huh?" He looked distraught. "Oh, uh, I can lend them my power." Then he paused. "But if I do it'll wipe me out."

"So will those vampires, if they survive," I noted while pointing at The Seven Glowing Fanged Ones. That would be a decent band name, if I did say so myself. "Do it, Warren."

He stepped over and put his hands on the PPD mage's shoulders and began his hilarious pygmy chant. I kept my mirth under control. Within a few seconds, the flow of light increased, rising above what Jasmine and Rachel had originally been outputting.

The vampire closest to us exploded, which was perfect because his energy smacked into the ones right behind him. That caused them to overload. They blew up too. This then cascaded back until all of the vampires blew up.

Warren collapsed. Rachel and Jasmine merely sat down, looking haggard and worn.

We were dead in the water.

So of course that's when the uber pixie decided to fly back around to check in on us.

Felicia and I took out our weapons and leveled them at the little dude. We weren't exactly in a position to do much, especially with my mages being drained and my wizard being asleep. If only our bullets could have gotten through the shield he had up, that would...

"*Turbo,*" I said through the connector, "*I don't suppose you could set our bullets to the same resonant frequency as his shield or something, could you?*"

Turbo gave me a funny look. *"What the heck are you talking about, Chief?"*

*"You know, like they do in all those space shows. Match the shield frequency of the other ship and you can shoot torpedoes and such straight through them. You've never heard of that?"*

*"No,"* he admitted, *"but it's an interesting idea. The only problem is that we're in the middle of the field here. I have no tools or anything. Besides, something like that would take about—"*

*"Three weeks, I know."* I sighed. *"Any suggestions, then? And don't say, 'Run.'"*

He began scratching his head as the uber pixie continued to study us.

"You there," he called down, pointing at Turbo, "you're a fucking pixie."

Turbo puffed out his chest. "Well, aren't you astute. Anything else you'd like to point out that's obvious, assnugget?"

I jolted at that. Since when did Turbo use language like that? He was one of only a few pixies I'd ever met that did *not* have a potty-mouth.

*"Did you just call him an assnugget?"* I asked in disbelief.

*"It's our default language,"* Turbo replied, turning a bit pink. That *did* seem to be true.

"Why are you with these assholes?" asked the uber pixie, seemingly not offended by Turbo's name-calling. "They're inferior to us. Even a dipshit like you has to know that."

"Of course I know that, turd tooth." He then grunted. "I'm their leader!"

*"You're our what?"* I said, blinking.

*"Roll with it, Chief."*

The uber zipped down quickly, looked over Turbo, and then zipped away again. It was so fast that it took me a moment to register the event.

"You're a lying sack of cocks," the uber said. He then pointed at me. "Officer Eaten Dix is the leader."

"Excuse me," I scoffed, feeling as though I'd been slapped. "My name is not Eaten Dix. It's Ian Dex, thank you very much."

"Oh, sorry," the uber said dramatically. "My information must have been incorrect." He held up a little scroll that he'd clearly just created from dust. "Oh, I see. It says that you just spend a lot of time eating dicks. I had that wrong."

I knew the little creep was trying to rile me up, so I just ignored his words. At least until I noticed that Rachel was giggling a little.

She stopped when I frowned at her.

Nice.

"See?" the uber said, pointing at Rachel. "Even she knows about your proclivity to chew the pipe, Officer Dix...sorry, Dex."

"Enough of you, worm fart," Turbo bellowed. "You are under arrest."

"Did you just call him a worm fart?" I asked aloud, thinking that wasn't even remotely worthwhile from the perspective of pixie language usage.

"I'm a little out of practice, Chief," he explained with a shrug.

The uber laughed at that.

"You can't defeat me," he said while continuing to chuckle. "Your mages are out of juice and that dong tugger of a wizard lying beside them is clearly spent. The only thing you've got going for you is that Officer Felacio Blowguys and you have guns, and those can't even penetrate my shields." The uber zoomed down again and poked Turbo on the chest, staring daggers at him. "Unless *you* are going to fight me, Turdblow?"

Obviously this guy, just like the other ubers we'd faced

over the last months, had dug up information on my entire crew. Typical bad guys didn't do this sort of thing. Over time, they got to know who you were, sure, but we'd never met any of these ubers, which meant they'd have to have done their research.

"What's your name?" I asked, hoping he'd stay close so I could reach out and snap him from the air. "Wad or Rash or Boil or something?"

He glared at me. "Rot."

"Twat?"

"No!" His eyes let out a little smoke. So he didn't like to be teased about his name. Weird, but okay. "I said my name is Rot."

"Ah, sorry." I took a casual step toward him. "So, let me ask you something, Crotch."

"It's Rot, fuckface," he hissed as he flew over and poked me on the nose.

I grabbed him.

# CHAPTER 20

*N*ow that should have been that, but if you could try to imagine what it may feel like to grab hold of twenty wasps who were all incredibly pissed off and who truly enjoyed stinging the shit out of anything and everything, you'd get the basic gist of how I was feeling at the moment.

"Don't let him go," Rachel cried as I wailed like a five-year-old who'd lost his Game Boy privileges for the night. "We can use his energy."

She grabbed my arm and reached out to Jasmine, who reached out and grabbed Warren's leg.

Just when I thought the searing pain in my hand couldn't be any worse, I got to experience the joy of becoming a fucking mage charger.

It felt like I'd stuck my finger in an outlet that connected directly to the electric company's Big Mama generator.

"It's working," exclaimed Rachel. "I'm already feeling much better."

"Me too," agreed Jasmine, "and Warren is waking up."

"Swell," I squeaked, holding on to Rot for dear life. Actually, it sounded more like, "Szzwwzzzzeezzzlllzzzllll."

My hand was starting to shine like I was about to cast a spell. I don't tend to cast spells, though, and that told me that I was about to feel a lot of pain. Soon.

"Rachel," I whimpered, nodding at my hand, "can I let go now? Pleassssse?"

Her eyes went wide, but she shook her head quickly.

"Don't just let him go. Throw him!"

She didn't have to tell me twice. I pulled away from her and launched that little fucker as hard as I could toward the closest building. I could only hope the collision would knock him out completely before he unleashed whatever the hell he'd been brewing while in my hand.

Unfortunately, he launched the spell just as he got within a few inches of the building.

A light show ensued that included a shockwave powerful enough to blow me back a few feet, like a strong wind in a crazy storm. I was still on my feet, but only barely.

Bricks shattered, taking off a chunk from the top of the building. We didn't have to worry about the fallout from those since we were far enough back, but the power of that explosion was something to behold.

"Ouch," I said at the realization that I'd just avoided the fate that poor building had suffered. "That's one powerful little dude."

Then I looked down and saw that my hand was badly charred.

Serena stepped over and started sending healing waves through my body.

*"Hey, man,"* said The Admiral, *"I know this isn't the best time to bring this up, but that's the hand I tend to spend a lot of time with. Do you think that maybe—"*

"*Shut up.*"

"*Right.*"

As Serena worked her healing magic, Turbo pointed at Rot, who was flying haphazardly away from us. He wasn't moving all that fast, either.

"Serena," I said, taking my hand from hers, "you need to track Rot. I'll heal on my own in time."

"Right."

She refocused on her tracking device and I turned to the mages and Warren.

"You all okay?"

"I'm nearly at full," Rachel said.

"Same here," agreed Jasmine.

Warren was obviously not back to full power, but he was conscious enough to say that he was fine. Honestly, we weren't likely to need much from him in the way of magic anyway. At least not offensive magic.

"Do you have enough power to tell us if normals are encased or not?" I asked him.

"Yeah, I can do that."

"Good enough. Let's get moving."

"*Ian, honey,*" Lydia said through the connector while Serena led the way after Rot, "*I just got word that Officer Benchley has been stabilized and is going into surgery.*"

"*Prognosis?*"

"*They're expecting him to pull through, but he'll be pretty weak, puddin'.*"

"*Understood,*" I said, noting the faces of grim determination on the rest of my team. "*Tell Chuck to stay with him. We'll get this damn pixie if it's the last thing we do.*"

I looked down again at my hand, thinking it may just be the last thing we do.

"*You got it, love muffin,*" she replied. "*Please be careful.*"

"*We always try to be,*" I answered and then shut down the

connection. "Griff will be fine," I noted, even though they'd all heard the conversation since Lydia hadn't used a direct-connection with me. "I'm sure of it."

"I hope you're right," said Warren. "Griff's the only mage who really gets what I do."

Rachel gave him a sidelong glance. "I understand what you do."

"So do I," agreed Jasmine.

"Sorry," he said. "I don't mean it like that. I meant that Griff and I have worked together for many hours. He has really tried to understand the nuances of wizardry, especially rune creation. It's kind of a hobby for him, I guess."

"Oh," Rachel and Jasmine said in unison.

We continued through the streets until Serena started to slow down. She was looking left and right until she finally came to a full stop. Then she smacked the side of the tracking unit and shook it a bit.

"Turbo," she said, "do you have any idea what this means?"

He glided over and stared down at the device.

"Hidden zone," he said and then tentatively flew forward, directly at the seam of bricks that connected the two buildings in front of us. He disappeared. "Yep," he repeated more loudly, "hidden zone."

We stepped through and found ourselves standing in an alley. Straight ahead sat a flight of stairs that were going down.

"I'm guessing he's down there?" I said, hoping Serena would say he wasn't.

"Yep."

Damn it.

"Okay," I sighed. "Well, at least he's drained of energy."

"I'm sure he's recovering quite quickly, Ian," noted Rachel. "We *are* in his lair."

I nodded grimly and started walking forward. Whatever that little bastard had in store for us was bound to be fun, especially now that I'd royally pissed him off.

"Super."

# CHAPTER 21

*W*e went slowly down the stairs, recognizing that Rot would expect us to follow him. Whether he knew we could track him or not was something we didn't yet know, but we saw no reason to chance it.

"Rune," announced Warren, pointing straight ahead. "Notification."

Well, that answered that.

"I don't suppose you can disable it without him knowing?" I asked hopefully.

"If we have an hour or so, I could try," he said, sounding miserable. "I mean I *can* disable it easily enough, but to make it so he doesn't know would take a lot more work."

I nodded.

Then I snapped my fingers. "Wait, will it tell him how many people hit it?"

"Yes," he answered slowly. "Each person who trips it will trigger an event and he'll pick it up."

"Okay, but what if I'm carrying someone over it and you're carrying someone over it?"

"That'd only be one event," he stated without hesitation.

"You're certain?"

Warren bit his lip and then knelt down to study the rune. He didn't get too close to it as he mumbled to himself. It sounded like he was counting, but now and then he'd say something like "hoozledul" and "dibblycoff," which were clearly not numbers…at least none that I'd ever heard.

"What's your plan?" Rachel asked as she sidled over.

"If I carry Serena over while she's holding Turbo, and Warren carries you—"

"Why wouldn't *you* carry *me* over and have Warren carry Serena over?" Her arms slowly crossed over her chest. Then she squinted at me. "In fact, why don't *I* carry *you* over and have Serena carry Warren over?"

There was no way I was getting out of this one. I'd placed my foot in my own mouth twice here. I know it, you know it, and Rachel damn well knew it.

So, I did the only thing I could do at that moment.

"Sorry."

She rolled her eyes. "Okay, fine, so we carry each other over. Then what?"

"Then we have it so Rot thinks there's only three of us, not seven."

"But he's seen us already," Jasmine chimed in. "Why would he think that we've suddenly lost three people?"

"He wouldn't," I replied with a smile, "but that's just it. It'll throw him off a little. He'll wonder if his runes have failed or if we sent part of our crew to come around a different way…" I paused and looked at their confused faces. "He'll feel just like you're feeling right now."

"Baffled?" asked Serena, from behind me.

"Yes."

"No, no," Turbo said, coming to my defense. "He's making sense here. Think about it. If you had seven people chasing you and you went into your house and locked the door, and then you saw three people walk past your surveillance camera, wouldn't you wonder where the others were?"

They all thought about it for a moment and then nodded slowly.

"There you go," I said. "It'll make Rot wonder where the rest of the squad is. That puts him slightly on his heels."

"Right," Rachel said. "I get it. You're just playing mind games with him. Okay, so what does that buy us exactly?"

"Hesitation," answered Serena. "Rot's overly confident, just like all the ubers we've run into. He prides himself on being fully in control. If some of us are missing, he's *not* fully in control."

I pointed at Serena. "Exactly. Whatever edge we can get, we'll take."

We'd faced these damn ubers enough times to know their egos were enormous. They got majorly ticked off when you messed with them, just like Rot did when I made fun of his name. Anything we could do to get the upper hand or put him off balance would only help us take him down faster.

"Chief," Warren said, waving me over, "if you look here you'll see that there are two spikes on this wheel. That's a single counter. If it were four spikes we'd be looking at unique energy signatures as opposed to a straight-up body count."

"Ooookay?"

"We can do the carrying each other over idea you mentioned," he explained. "Unless, of course, he's got these things all over the place down here, then all bets are off."

"Right." I turned to the team. "Okay, so who wants to carry whom?"

A couple of minutes later we were standing on the other side of the rune. Rachel had successfully carried me and Turbo over. I was honestly rather impressed, and more than a little turned on.

*"Me too,"* agreed The Admiral.

At least he was talking about my actual girlfriend this time.

Warren had tried to lift Serena but failed, so she picked him up and walked across. Then Felicia swung Jasmine up in her arms and strode across like it was nothing.

*"Now, there's a fantasy."*

"Perv," said Rachel.

*"Do you think she heard me?"* The Admiral twitched.

*"No, idiot."*

Or, wait…was *that* how she always knew what I was thinking whenever there were hot chicks about who were doing things that would make my libido heat up a few points? I immediately realized that was a dumb thing to think. First off, no. Secondly, if she *could* hear my dick talking to me, she'd have overheard a lot more of our conversations over the years than the basics. And last, it didn't take dick-telepathy to know what I was thinking whenever there were babes around. I was pretty much an open book.

"Okay," said Jasmine, interrupting my thoughts, "so Rot should expect that there's only part of our group coming through here. Now what?"

"Now we split up and find him," I answered. "Whoever spots him first, let the others know and we'll get it sorted out."

We broke off into groups, with Jasmine and Felicia heading left, Serena, Warren, and Turbo going to the right, and me and Rachel walking straight forward.

Each step was measured and quiet. The last thing we wanted to do was tip the guy off. Rachel was carefully scanning for runes, and I could only hope the others on my team were, too.

I was scanning the area with Boomy out. My goal was to protect Rachel at all costs.

One of the problems with being in a relationship with your partner was running into things like what had happened between Griff and Chuck. I couldn't even imagine the grief Chuck was suffering through right now. Looking at Rachel, I would be tearing myself up inside if she were to be seriously injured. That brought back memories of her being kidnapped in London. Memories of that emotional rollercoaster sucked.

Did she feel the same about me? I mean, she *did* say that she had originally left to join the London PPD because she couldn't stand being around me when bad things happened. But I thought that was more to do with the valkyries wanting to bone me than anything else.

"*Rachel,*" I said with some trepidation via a direct-connection, "*I want to ask you something and I want you to be completely honest with me.*"

"*Sounds serious,*" she replied. "*Go ahead.*"

"*It* is *serious, so please just answer me honestly here.*"

She stopped walking and looked at me with a face of concern.

"*Okay, Ian. What is it?*"

"*Can you hear it when my dick talks?*"

# CHAPTER 22

*R*achel never answered the question. She merely looked at me as though judging whether or not we would be sharing the same bed again…ever.

The worry over the possibility that she may be able to hear the communications between me and The Admiral *did* seem to shut him up though.

We continued our sneaking until we finally walked into a large room. It looked kind of like a school gymnasium. There were basketball hoops, floor mats, a small set of bleachers, and six gigantic pixies who were hovering just above the ground at the far end of the room.

I did a double-take.

"Are those things real?" I heard Warren gasp from our left. Then he whispered, "Sorry."

*"Check to make sure they don't have normals in them,"* I instructed.

*"In those things?"* he replied. *"Seriously?"*

After I gave him a look, he did his little spell and shook his head.

Thank goodness for small favors.

I glanced to our right and saw Felicia and Jasmine coming into the room as well. That meant our paths led here. So much for all that 'carrying each other over the rune' crap.

Regardless, I was having one hell of a time coming to terms with the size of the pixies in front of us.

As one, my entire team walked toward the oversized supers like we were zombies. Honestly, I could only imagine that this was what a moth must feel like right before it got fried into oblivion by one of those bug zapper things. And no matter how much I felt that this was stupid, I just kept walking.

"They can't be real, right?" Rachel asked out of the side of her mouth. "It'd be silly."

"No," I argued, "what's silly is that we're still moving toward the damn things."

"Valid point. Why are we doing that?"

"Because we're in disbelief, I'm hoping?"

The beasties were easily ten feet tall, if not more. They looked adorably evil with their fluttering wings and bobtail hairdos. Well, the males anyway. The females had more of a short cut going that was set off by dark eye makeup.

Sexy.

*"Never been with a pixie before,"* The Admiral whispered. *"Normally, that'd be pretty disturbing, but these babes are huge."*

I waited to hear "perv" or "freak" or something else from Rachel, but she said nothing. So that meant that she *couldn't* hear our discussions. Right?

Damn it.

As one, we all reached out and touched the pixies on their stomachs.

Why? I had no fucking idea.

But it turned out to be a bad move. Of course, you probably assumed that already.

All of the pixies backhanded us in unison with a

resounding "thwack," flinging us back across the room. It was one major wallop. I'd been hit more times than your average boxer, but never like that. And from a *pixie*, no less!

I groaned and rubbed my jaw as I pushed up to one elbow.

"Seems they're real," I said.

"Definitely real," agreed Rachel. "And, yet, we couldn't have just admired them from afar."

The ground shook slightly as a massive thumping sounded.

It happened again.

I glanced over and saw that the ginormous creatures were slowly heading our way, fanning out in a one-to-one scenario. I did the math and it wasn't good. We were definitely going to be down one wizard when this was all said and done. There was no way Warren could handle one of these guys, even if Turbo backed him up.

"Try fire, ice, energy, bullets, knives," I blathered as quickly as I could. "Rub their bellies if you have to..." I paused. "No wait, that didn't work. You know what I mean. Fight!"

Boomy was essentially useless, which really sucked because my particular pixie had a whip, and she was really good at aiming it. Fortunately, I was very agile, so I had successfully dodged every attempt she made at splitting me in two.

Rachel was firing energy pulses at her attacker, Jasmine went with fireballs, Felicia shot and then threw her knife, Serena was dodging and kicking at hers, and Warren whimpered and ran around, trying his damndest to escape. Turbo didn't have a pixie of his own to battle, but he was trying his best to protect Warren.

"Hey," I yelled out at my pixie, "why don't you put that whip down and fight like a man?"

"I guess because I'm not a man," she answered in a deep, booming voice. "Now, stay still so I can flay the skin from your body, you fucking vampire!"

Oh, good. These could talk.

Then, I frowned and stood up straight. She must have noticed the change in my demeanor, because she paused her attack.

"Why would you assume I was a vampire?" I asked through gritted teeth.

She shrugged. "The suit, the hair, the good looks, and the way you walk."

"Oh," I said. "Well, I'm *not* a vampire. I'm an amalgamite."

"A what?"

"Amalgamite," I repeated. She squinted. "I'm a combination of races, essentially."

"Ahhh," she said, and then asked, "So is your mom Snow White or something? Maybe your dads are like Wolfy, Fangy, Fucky, Pumpy, Boney, Screwy, and Sticker?"

"That doesn't even make sense," I countered. "And, no."

She laughed and raised her whip again.

I took the chance to run right at her. If I'd had a second to think logically about this plan of action, I probably would have gone a different way, but there was no turning back now.

The whip cracked over my head, threatening to burst my eardrums.

I slid under her.

And before you start wondering, I did *not* look up.

When I got through to the other side, I spun and jumped onto her back, trying to get her in a rear naked choke. Her neck was as thick as an oak tree, though, meaning I couldn't even get a grip.

Out of pure desperation, I curled my fingers and dug them into her shoulder.

She growled and shook me away, dropping me to the wood floor in a heap. It hurt. But there was a mass of dust that fell from the "wound."

I'd torn a piece of her away.

"Hand to hand," I yelled. "Get in close and start ripping them apart!"

This was all Felicia needed to hear in order to turn into wolf form again. Her claws would make quick work of a beast like this.

My pixie spun around and raised up her foot, bringing it down at my head with a vengeance. I rolled out of the way, scooted down, and then grabbed her Achilles, ripping it out in one smooth motion.

The bitch fell forward with a cry.

That gave me enough time to jump up and charge at the pixie who was chasing Warren.

I dived through the air and crashed right into its knees, dislodging the dust like I was breaking bones. The dude tumbled over, cursing me as he tried to get a grip on me. But Warren had picked up a baseball bat from one of the nearby bins and began swinging it at his fallen foe like the damn thing owed him money.

Unfortunately, none of this was going to be permanent.

My pixie was already filling in the dust back on the back of her leg. She'd be fully functioning again in no time. And even though Felicia was making great headway on her pixie, she'd be tired out before getting through a second one.

"I know what to do," announced Serena, "but I need time, and I need Turbo."

"Yeah, there's a problem with that," I yelled back. "We're outnumbered."

That's when the miraculous vision of Chuck burst into the room. Black hat, black jacket, hate on his face, and holding two double-barreled, sawed-off shotguns.

# CHAPTER 23

*C*huck strode purposefully up to the pixie that Serena was fighting, stuck the ends of the shotgun into its stomach, and fired.

"Chuck," I called out, "that's not going to—"

Two massive holes blasted out the back of the pixie, nearly cutting it in two.

"—work."

*"Griff's out of surgery,"* he said through the connector. *"He's going to be fine. He had about twenty seconds of consciousness before dozing back off and he said that we needed to get close in to whatever we're facing in order to bypass the shield."*

So that's why my digging into them directly was working. I was through the shield. Same with Warren's bat.

*"You heard the man,"* I commanded. *"Get in close and do your damndest."*

*"Still won't stop them from healing themselves,"* Serena argued. *"Turbo, follow me!"*

Actually, my feeling was that if we tore these damn things apart fast enough, they'd not have a chance to heal. Just like when we shot the hands off the apes. Of course, Rot did seem to be going out of his way to improve his creations at every turn, so who knew what was in store for us at this point.

Just as I was about to instruct everyone to aim for the hands, I noticed something very odd.

The dust from the pixie that Chuck had shot at close range had attached to my fallen pixie. She was in the process of fixing her Achilles, but the dust finished the job for her. And then, to make things really fun, the dust started attaching to the rest of her body, where it proceeded to heal her.

She was growing.

"*Uh, guys,*" I said while pointing a shaky finger.

Rachel yelled out a spell as she flew through the air with her hand out like she was a superhero. Her fist connected with her pixie and an explosion of energy tore a massive hole right through it.

Again, the dust hit my pixie.

Again, it grew bigger.

"*Uh...guys,*" I said even louder.

Felicia was attached to her pixie. She was clawing, biting, and doing everything she could to tear the poor thing to shreds. I know I shouldn't have felt any sympathy for it, but Felicia was vicious.

My pixie grew even more.

"*Seriously, guys.*"

A flash of light came from my right, over by a set of darkened windows. Jasmine wasn't known to be much of a fighter, but she was often quite clever. She had thrown up a fireworks spell, which caused her pixie to get distracted. This gave Jasmine the time to step inside and stick a timed spell on its leg. When she'd run away, the pixie was short one limb.

And there went my pixie's size again.

"Guys," I hollered without the connector, "my fucking pixie is getting bigger every time the dust hits her!"

Apparently, my pixie noticed this as well because she got a nice sinister grin, stood up, and started running to all of the dust piles. Each one she hit merged with her immediately and she grew even more.

"*Oh boy,*" Rachel gulped. "*Didn't see that coming.*"

"*Nope.*"

But it got worse.

My pixie stepped down on Rachel's fallen pixie, smashing its head in a horrific visual of disturbing death.

She grew.

This gave us a slight reprieve, though, because the other pixies had caught on to what was happening and they didn't like it any more than we did. Different reasons, obviously, but we shared an eventual outcome. Still, we'd let them fight it out as we figured out the next steps.

"Everyone, get over here," I called, running to a spot on the floor where there was no dust. "We have to figure this shit out, and fast."

The only two who hadn't joined me were Serena and Turbo. They were off doing something that Serena felt was important to stopping these beasts. Seeing that she'd always been deathly accurate about things in the past, I let her do her thing.

"Glad you're with us, Chuck," I noted. "And *very* happy to hear that Griff is going to be okay."

Everyone gave him a pat on the arm or shoulder to show support. Jasmine full-on hugged the guy.

I looked past him and saw that my pixie was nearly twice her original size. All the other big pixies had been destroyed now, but my pixie used their remaining dust to grow and grow. Her height hadn't gone up as much, but her physique was bulging and her arms were getting longer. The only reason I could think of that would make sense for that was it allowing her to keep us at bay.

"Okay, okay," I said. "We don't have much time. That pixie is getting huge and I don't think she's going to make it easy for us to get in close."

Felecia growled in agreement.

"But we have numbers on our side," noted Rachel. "She's only got two arms."

"Which means we need two volunteers to be at the receiving end of those arms," I replied soberly. "And while I hate to say it, those two volunteers need to be mages."

Jasmine and Rachel looked at me like I had lost my mind.

"Sorry, guys, but it makes the most sense." I motioned at myself, Felicia, and Chuck. "We have guns." Then I pointed at Warren. "He's got…" I paused, pursed my lips, realized that Warren would make the perfect fodder here, and then looked back at Jasmine and Rachel. "Okay, so I only need *one* of you mages to volunteer."

"But—" started Warren.

"I could have you on the brute force team," I stated, clearly lying so as not to hurt his feelings, "but this thing isn't a skeleton." I was referring to the time he'd torn those zombie skeletons limb from limb. It had been quite the sight, but there was a huge difference between fighting a bag of bones and facing off against a massive pixie. "So unless you've—"

He held up his bat, tapping it slowly against his palm. I glanced over at the pixie he'd demolished with his clubbing and changed my mind.

"Okay, so it's back to the two mages."

"Ian, you have to realize that—"

"That you two are going to get crushed, Rachel?" I interrupted. "I realize that it's a possibility, and it sucks." I pointed at my pixie. "But if you go after her hands with an energy pulse like you did a couple minutes back against your pixie, you may be able to mitigate the hit. That will give us enough time to take out the damn thing's midsection." I glanced at Warren. "If we can get it on the ground, Skull Thumper here will finish the job."

"I love it when you give me tough names like that," mused Warren, clearly not catching my sarcasm.

"Question," said Jasmine while pointing at my pixie. "Why is she carrying dust to the middle of the room?"

That was odd. She was keeping a wary eye on us as she pushed a mass of dust around. I would have expected it to make her larger and larger, but it was as if she was saving it for something.

Oh shit.

"She's going to use it for healing," Chuck announced before I could. "That's not good."

"It really isn't," agreed Jasmine.

"Time to fight before she—"

I was too late.

She turned and grinned at us, signaling she was ready for battle.

It was go time.

# CHAPTER 24

*W*e moved out onto the gymnasium floor, getting ourselves into an umbrella pattern with Rachel and Jasmine at the top.

They didn't look happy about their position in this battle.

Neither was I, truth be told.

I'd seen what had happened to Griff and what Chuck had gone through. I honestly had no desire for Rachel and I to go through it, too. But I couldn't show favoritism. When we were on the job, she was an officer just like any other. Frankly, I hated putting any of them in danger, but that was all part of being the chief and, like it or not, Rachel and Jasmine were the best choice for taking the hands off this pixie.

*"Everyone ready?"* I asked through the connector.

I saw nods out of the corner of my eye.

*"Okay, Rachel,"* I sighed. *"You're on."*

She stepped forward and put her hands on her hips, giving the pixie the onceover. Then she slowly started shaking her head.

The pixie grimaced, looking concerned.

"What?" challenged the beast in her booming voice.

"Nothing," Rachel replied. "It's just that you look ridiculous."

The pixie studied herself for a moment.

"Why?"

"Well, your skirt doesn't really match your shirt," began Rachel. "Your hair is...well, I don't even know what to say about that, and you're not even wearing shoes."

We were all slowly fanning out while waiting for just the right moment. My guess was it'd be soon, seeing that Rachel was clearly already pushing some buttons. She excelled at that.

"Oh, like you're one to talk," the pixie retaliated. "Blond hair, blue eyes, brown leather that's so tight it looks painted on." The pixie scoffed. "I may be dressed eccentrically, but at least I don't look like a two-bit whore."

"Oooh," I groaned to myself while wincing. "That was the wrong thing to say."

"Same goes for your dainty little friend, too," noted the pixie, clearly not recognizing the danger she was putting herself in. "So you're a whore and she's a slut." She nodded proudly. "Yes, that about sums it up, wouldn't you say?"

Rachel and Jasmine took off so fast that it made Rot look slow in comparison.

They were both in superhero flight-mode, with their fists out. The problem was that they didn't have any glowing stuff going on with their hands. In their rage, they'd neglected to power up.

Translation: They were fucked.

"Go, go, go!" I yelled.

The entire team swarmed in on the big pixie, ready to shoot, claw, bite, and...swing a bat. Yeah, okay, so Warren's contribution to the battle wasn't great, but if he ever got to the pixie's head, we'd be in business.

Rachel flew back the way she came, smacking into the far wall with a thud. Jasmine hit next to her a second later.

I couldn't look.

Once I was in close enough, I jumped up and stuck Boomy right on the pixie's elbow. The bullet nearly tore her arm in half, which was enough to elicit a shriek, but dust pulled up from the pile behind her in a jiffy. She was healed before I hit the ground.

Chuck had blown off one of her knees with his shotguns, but it was fixed just as fast.

This clearly wasn't going to work and the pixie knew it.

She reached down and snapped up Warren, bringing him to eye level. To his credit, he pulled the bat up over his head and bonked her right on the nose with it. Her eyes grew dark and he dropped the bat. It landed right on Chuck's foot. From that height, it was enough to cause Chuck to yell, "Fuck!"

"Uh…" started Warren, looking like he was about to piddle. "If it means anything to you, I rather like your skirt and shirt combination. It's eccentric, sure, but that just makes you interesting."

"Thank you," she said before throwing him back to meet the wall near Rachel and Jasmine. "I like your outfit, too."

She reached down for me next, but I dived out of the way and shot her toe off.

No, it wasn't doing permanent damage, but at least it was hurting her. Of course, that just proved to piss her off even more, which wasn't a great thing.

"*Ian,*" Serena piped up, "*we have things going here, but you're going to have to hold on.*"

"*What are you talking about?*" I asked her while dodging yet another swipe from the pixie's massive hand. "*You said you had a plan, but you never told us what it was.*"

Chuck fired his shotguns again and again. It was buying us time, but that wouldn't last.

"*There's an industrial vacuum over here,*" she explained. "*I saw it when we came in from the other entrance. Turbo has been working on making it run even faster.*"

"*Uh huh,*" I groaned after getting thrown into the bleachers. That hurt. "*A vacuum.*"

"*What does a vacuum do, Ian?*"

"*Same thing my life does most of the time,*" I answered. "*It sucks.*"

"*Specifically dust and dirt, yes,*" she said.

I sat up and cracked my neck, waiting for the spasm in my back to die down.

"*Wait a second,*" I said once Serena's words fully hit home. "*You're talking about treating this pixie like she's just a big-ass dust bunny?*"

"*Precisely.*"

"*Well, all right then.*"

I jumped off the bleachers as Felicia flew toward me. I ducked. She bounced off one of the seats and flew right back into the fray. Oh to have *that* level of agility. I was more agile than the average person by far, but a genetically enhanced werewolf such as Felicia was an insanely powerful springboard.

"*Could use some magic here, too,*" Serena added.

I glanced over at Rachel and Jasmine, who were both sitting up and rubbing their heads.

"*Rachel?*"

"*Yeah, yeah, yeah,*" she replied. "*We'll help her, Ian. You guys keep that pixie busy.*"

There was no need to tell me twice.

I turned and ran toward the pixie with Boomy in hand and menace on my mind.

CHAPTER 25

*I* shook my head and found that I was again looking up at the ceiling in the gymnasium. I didn't even remember getting clobbered that time.

Felicia was getting up on one side of me and Chuck was rousing on the other. Obviously, the massive pixie had gotten the better of all three of us simultaneously.

*Thump.*

Uh oh.

I sat up as my head swam and saw that she was heading over to finish the job. Unfortunately, when I reached for Boomy I found that he was gone.

"Huh?" I said aloud while frowning. "Where the fuck did I—"

*Thump.*

No time to worry about it.

"Chuck," I said, pushing him, "get up. Felicia, you okay?"

She growled in reply, and it wasn't an angry growl either. It was one of those I-think-I-just-got-hit-by-a-train kind of growls.

*Thump.*

"Come on, guys," I said, jumping to my feet. "Get up now!"

The huge pixie actually stopped beside the three of us and went, "Muwahahahaha!" She sounded like a total tyrant, and that irked me for some reason.

I spun around just as she was about to stomp us into oblivion and gave her a very firm look as I wagged an admonishing finger up at her.

She halted, lowered her foot carefully, and blinked at me.

"You're not a nice person," I said flatly. "Not nice at all."

Her features changed suddenly to look very pouty. She dropped her head a little and glanced away.

"I…" she started. "You know what? You're right."

"Yes, and…" I paused and lowered my finger. "I am?"

"Yeah." Her eyes flashed and her foot came back up. "I'm *not* a nice person."

"Shit!"

We all jumped and rolled and screamed and yelled, but that pixie had one big-ass foot.

I dodged it.

Chuck dodged.

Felicia wasn't so lucky. She yelped like a puppy getting a rabies shot as the pixie's foot crushed down on her leg.

Like a shot, I launched at the pixie's calf and started tearing at it as Felicia limped away. Chuck shot the pixie's foot clean off. She shrieked and started to fall forward. The dust was rushing over to heal her, but since she wasn't right on top of it, we had a few seconds between each hit.

"Keep shooting," I demanded.

Chuck went to oblige my request, but she swiped at him and knocked him on his ass. Then she kicked me away.

When I looked up from my place on the court, I found her crawling back toward her healing pile of sand.

That's when the sound of an industrial vacuum went on.

It was so powerful that the pixie's healing dust started zooming out of the room in a stream.

"Nooo," she cried as she tried desperately to get over to what was left of it.

Whatever Turbo had done to that vacuum, it was impressive. So much so that it was starting to pull me, Chuck, and Felicia along, too. Worse, I saw Boomy across the way, and he was wobbling.

"Oh crap!" I yelled as I did my best to run toward my beloved gun. "Come to daddy, Boomy. Come to daddy!"

Boomy didn't listen.

He simply lifted up and started flying toward the vacuum, being sucked away into a set of blades that would forever change his personality.

Don't judge me. I talk to my dick, remember?

"Stop the fans," I cried. "Stop the fucking fans."

"Don't worry," Rachel yelled out. "I snagged your precious gun before he went in. It's called magic. You have the ability. Learn to use it."

Well, someone was being a little snippy.

"Thank you," I replied heavily, but there was no way she could have heard me from here, and I wasn't speaking through the connector. I opened a channel. *"Thank you."*

Felicia was having a tough time keeping herself from getting pulled into the stream as well, but she was a lot bigger than Boomy so I was able to get to her and pull her beside the bleachers where the suction was less problematic.

"Do you need an emergency portal?" I asked.

She growled a "No."

"You're not just being stoic?"

Another growl.

"Okay, I'm going to help Chuck."

I stood up and saw that Chuck had made his way over to

the fallen pixie and was preparing to make her one with the vacuum.

He had jumped on her back and pointed both shotgun barrels right at the back of her head. The blasts sounded simultaneously, sending a river of sand toward the vacuum. But that didn't stop Chuck.

He just kept firing and firing and reloading and firing again. He didn't stop until there was nothing left of that pixie but a pile of dust that was speedily being sucked away.

He collapsed a second later and was moving toward the vacuum.

*"You can slow that thing down now,"* I commanded through the connector. *"The pixie is dead."*

The sound of suction lowered and Chuck stopped moving toward the doors, but the dust was still making its way toward the exit. Warren was rousing now and looked to be searching for his bat.

I got to Chuck and rolled him over. He was fine, just exhausted.

"How are you feeling?"

"Sated," he answered.

"We still have the uber to get after," I reminded him while helping him back to his feet. "He's the one responsible for injuring Griff, remember?"

He nodded dully as I walked him over to where Warren was still fumbling around. Clearly my wizard had gotten his bell rung pretty hard. So had I, but I healed way faster than he could ever hope to...unless he had a shot of elixir, of course.

"Warren," I said, jolting him from his search. He spun around and swung at me. I caught the punch in my hand and he froze. "The pixie is dead."

"Oh," he mumbled. "Sorry."

"It's okay," I replied. "I appreciate your instincts, actually.

Just have a seat and recover for a few minutes while we figure out our next steps."

Both Warren and Chuck sat down.

"Serena," I said through the connector, "*Felicia is injured and needs your healing hands, please.*"

"*Is she okay?*" asked a frantic Jasmine as she ran out into the gymnasium, keeping to the wall to avoid the continuing suction. Yes, it was less, but being directly in front of that vacuum would still give quite a pull to someone Jasmine's size. "*Where is she?*"

"*By the bleachers,*" I answered. "*I pulled her over there to get her away from the vacuum.*"

Serena ran out a couple seconds later, bolting straight across without too much effort. She *was* bigger than Jasmine, though.

"*Rachel,*" I said in a direct-connection, "*are you all right?*"

"*I'm fine,*" she replied. "*You?*"

"*Exhausted.*"

"*Yeah.*"

CHAPTER 26

The last thing I wanted to do at this point was walk right into another one of Rot's traps.

"Everyone, rest up as quickly as you can," I said, realizing that made little sense. "You know what I mean."

"No need," Chuck announced, pulling forth a somewhat dented flask from his jacket. "I stopped by my condo and picked up one of Griff's energy elixirs."

Nice.

"Does he make a lot of those?" asked Warren.

"No, we buy them for when we're, uh…" He looked up, blushing. "Let's just say we buy them. Anyway, they really give you renewed energy, and this one happens to have some healing powers, too. It only takes a sip, so don't overdo it."

He offered it to me first, but I motioned him to give it to the rest of my crew. They all needed it more than I did, especially Felicia. If it got back to me empty, that was fine. I'd be in tiptop shape within a few minutes.

Speaking of Felicia, she was back to her human self and looked to be on the mend. Having Serena around for healing was fantastic. It took a bit out of her, though, so it was a good thing Chuck had fetched that elixir.

I moved over to Serena and tapped on the tracking device.

"Where's our little bundle of joy now?"

She held up her finger and took a swig from the flask. The effect was instantaneous. Her posture improved, the coloring came back to her face, and her eyes watered slightly.

"Whoa," she said, "that's a spicy meatball!"

I frowned at her as she handed the flask over to Felicia.

"Anyway," Serena said, flicking on the device, "looks like he's straight through that door."

She stood up, as did everyone else. I was the only one still seated. While they all had their energy back, I needed a couple of minutes.

Rachel handed me the flask. There was plenty left. I took a swig and felt an immediate rush of life. It was like drinking thirty shots of espresso one after the other, but without the jitters and likely heart attack.

"Okay," I said, feeling a million times better, "I know you all want to go in there and whip that little creep's ass, but I'm really not interested in seeing what else he has in store for us." I shook the flask. "This is great, but it won't last forever."

"What do you suggest, then?" said Rachel.

"I'm not sure, to be honest," I answered.

*Flashes.*

The word echoed in my head, causing me to stagger slightly.

"You okay, Chief?" Chuck asked as he helped stabilize me.

"Yeah, yeah, I'm fine," I replied after a moment. "Just got one of Gabe's fun words bouncing in my head."

Jasmine looked at me. "Which one?"

"*Flashes.*" I studied the area. "Any idea what I could use

to..." I paused and noticed that there was still a smattering of pixie dust on the floor. "Never mind."

I walked over and started gathering the dust until it covered my palm.

Then the world went dark.

# CHAPTER 27

"You know what to do?" came a whisper out of whomever it was I was inhabiting this time.

I tried to place it, but between it being a whisper and me being inside of the head that was speaking, it was tough. It's like hearing a recording of your own voice for the first time. You can't believe it's you talking.

We were standing in a cave, but not the same one I'd seen when I was looking to destroy Rex the werewolf. This was in the mountains somewhere. I could sense a breeze.

"Of course I know, ball biter," said the pixie in front of me. It wasn't Rot. "Torment and kill. It's not fucking brain surgery."

"It also won't be as easy as you expect," said another voice, but I couldn't see who that belonged to. "You will find these people are rather resourceful."

"Ooooh," the pixie mocked. "Look at me shaking."

"Sorry to interrupt, Jibbs," another pixie said, flying in. It was Rot. He looked a little younger. "There is an army approaching."

So this pixie named Jibbs was in charge now and Rot was one of his commanders?

"Good," said Jibbs. "I'm ready to kill." He then flashed a set of warning eyes at whomever I was inhabiting and added, "Stay out of the way and learn what pixies can *really* do."

He fled from the cave and out into the night.

My shell followed along with someone else. Again, I couldn't see who it was, but I had the feeling they were irrelevant to my host. I couldn't quite dig into the thoughts of the person I was in, but the general feeling was that *everyone* was expendable, as long as it fed the ultimate purpose, whatever the hell that was.

Jibbs started throwing out dust, which allowed him to create vampires and wolves, much like Rot had been doing to me and my crew. Rot was also casting these little spells, but his creatures were not as robust. They were more like jackals and vultures. Still annoying and deadly, but nothing compared to what I'd seen him create in the present.

"Attack," commanded Jibbs.

The dust-beasts charged the oncoming army and mayhem ensued. Screams and shrieks could be heard reverberating through the valley.

Again, the emotions of my host were flat. Even though lives were being lost out there, there was nothing but the feeling of a cold-minded individual who just wanted to test the results of a hypothesis. There was no elation at the battle or dread or anything. It was just a feeling of factuality. "Is Jibbs sufficient for my purposes?" was what I felt was being asked.

The army lost a quarter of its soldiers before all of the creatures Jibbs had made turned back to dust.

"Fuck," said the little pixie. "I must do more than this."

Rot held up a hand. "May I suggest that we think outside the box?"

This caught my host's attention. His interest was definitely piqued.

Jibbs didn't feel the same.

"Of course not," Jibbs admonished his inferior. "You are nothing but a weathered beast, Rot. I am in charge here."

"But you're going to lose this battle," Rot retaliated. "My ideas will—"

"Stop your insolence before I kill you where you stand," Jibbs hissed with nefarious intent.

"Fuck you, Jibbs," Rot replied, crossing his arms. "You're nothing but an overbearing cum bubble. I've had it with you and your half-assed attempts at being tough."

"Is that right?" Jibbs scowled.

"Yep."

"And what, pray tell, does your little vomit fondling ass intend to do about it?"

Rot puffed out his chest and yelled, "I demand a Joke-Off!"

CHAPTER 28

The world snapped back to the present and I fell
over. My crew rushed over and helped me back to
a seated position.

"What happened?" said Rachel. "You blinked and then
fell over."

"I saw what needs to be done," I answered as Chuck
handed me the flask of energy. It woke me up again. "I have
to Joke-Off."

Everyone stood up straight and stared at me with shock
in their eyes.

"Here?" said everyone in unison.

*"Yeah, dude,"* agreed The Admiral, *"even I think that's a little
weird. I mean, I'm up for it if you are, but could we at least ask
Chuck, Warren, and Turbo to step out while we start stroking?"*

"I said *JOKE-OFF*," I clarified.

"Ohhhh," the group replied, but only Turbo looked to
understand what that meant.

"I haven't seen one of those in years, Chief," said our little
pixie. "They're pretty tough. Actually, I can't see how you

could win. Pixies grow up training for these in the event they should ever happen."

"Oh."

"What is it, exactly?" asked Felicia.

Turbo landed on Warren's shoulder and started to explain.

"Traditionally, it's when two pixies are at odds about something grave. It's the equivalent of a human duel. The difference is that pixies use words instead of swords or pistols."

*Words.*

I stumbled again.

"Damn it," I groaned, grabbing my head. "It's one thing that Gabe gives me these fucking power word things, but do they have to screw me up every time they make themselves known?"

Rachel frowned at me. "Huh?"

"Nothing. Look, the last one Gabe hooked me up with was *Words*. I don't know what it's supposed to do, but I'm guessing it's because of this shit I'm facing."

"Wait," said Rachel. "How would Gabe know you'd be facing a pixie?"

"I know, right?" I answered with a shake of my head. "Fact is that he knows a lot more than he's been telling me. So do the damn Directors. But I can't get anything out of anybody that's much help." I then sighed. "I suppose Gabe is at least giving me *something* to work with to combat these fucking ubers."

"True," agreed Rachel, "but it'd be nice to know why."

"Tell me about it," I grunted. "Anyway, I'm guessing that this *Words* skill, or whatever you call it, that Gabe gave me is going to allow me to challenge Rot to a Joke-Off."

Turbo flew over and hovered in front of my face. He looked more serious than I'd ever seen him before.

"Chief," he said carefully, "this is next-level stuff with pixies. There's no backing out of it from either side."

"There's no backing out of anything when you're a PPD officer, Turbo," I pointed out. "It's the nature of the job."

He gripped his hat tighter.

"The point is that the rest of the officers can't join you in this."

"What?" I asked him.

"Fuck that," snorted Rachel. "If he gets in trouble—"

"Then he'll lose, Rachel," Turbo said.

"Well, what the hell does that mean?"

Turbo swallowed hard while looking at her.

"It'll mean whatever Rot wants it to mean." He then put his eyes back on me. "Chief, he may decide to kill you or have you join his side. It could be anything, and you can't go against the outcome either. Joke-Offs run deep in the pixie community." He looked down. "This is serious stuff, Chief."

Great.

So here I was about to go into a room to face a little pixie in a battle of words and possibly never come out, or worse, end up as his second-in-command and be forced to kill my own crew.

That shook me to the core.

"I won't serve under the pixie," I stated flatly. "I have no problem dying.... Okay, so I have quite a big problem with dying, but I'll do that before I serve alongside that dude."

"You don't understand," Turbo stammered. "This is heavy magic. You'll be transfixed and will have *no* way out of it."

"Oh," I said after a few moments. "Well, that sucks."

Turbo pulled out his little data pad and started typing away, saying "hmmm" and "huh" more than once. Obviously he was doing some type of research. Maybe there was a PixieNet or something I didn't know about?

"Okay," he said with some effort. "I guess it's been a lot

longer since I've seen a Joke-Off than I'd thought." He let out a slow breath. "Looks like you *can't* go in there alone, Chief. You need a pixie with you to set the terms and to act as the judge and referee." He scrolled up a few times. "Well, Rot could have a pixie, too, but since you're the challenger, you can use your own if you'd prefer. Personally, I'd be fine if you elected to go with his guy instead of me, but—"

"I'd rather have you in there, Turbo," I said, interrupting him. "Now, if there's anything else in the rulebook that you want me to know, *now* would be the time."

He fanned through the online document, scanning through it faster than I could likely read a single sentence of it. I wasn't what you'd call "book smart."

"Nothing I can see, Chief," he said. "There are basic rules that we have to follow, but those will be laid out once you throw down the gauntlet."

"Assuming he doesn't have more monsters in there to stop me," I mumbled.

"No, he can't," said Turbo.

"What?"

"Once you challenge him, he has to shut everything else down and face you one on one."

I furrowed my brow. "You're shitting me."

"Nope."

That's when a thought struck. "What about *Words*?" I asked. "It's kind of me, but not really. Will that be considered cheating?"

"Can this *Words* thing exist without you?"

I glanced around when *Words* said, "*No.*" I looked up at Turbo. "Nope."

"Then you're all set."

"Super."

CHAPTER 29

he rest of the squad stayed behind. Turbo made me disconnect the connector and everything, noting that if I was deemed to be cheating in any way, shape, or form, I'd be immediately considered the loser of the event.

I couldn't have that.

Turbo was on my shoulder as I pushed open the door where Rot was supposedly waiting for my crew.

It was a dark room that was considerably smaller than the gymnasium, at least the part I could see. There were stacks of boxes on the right side that went up to the ceiling, though, so it wasn't until I stepped past the last row that I heard the sound of a low growl.

I turned to my right and saw two very large, very orange, glowing eyes. Under them was a long snout with massive fangs. It was attached to a head that had a long neck. That, in turn, connected to a body that came equipped with wings.

It was a drake.

Sometimes I wished I couldn't see so well in the dark.

"Yikes," I whispered.

The drake began rising up. It wasn't the size of a full dragon or anything, but it was enough to be pretty damn powerful. I wasn't really looking forward to fighting it.

"Challenge him," Turbo said.

"Him?" I answered, pointing at the drake. "I'd really rather not."

"No, Chief. I'm talking about Rot."

*Words.*

I nearly fell over with that one.

"Goddamn it," I yelled mostly at myself. "Quit fucking doing that!"

"Doing what, Chief?"

"Not you," I said back before bellowing, "I demand a Jack Off!"

The drake froze and blinked at me, saying, "Huh?"

"It's *Joke-Off*, Chief, remember?"

"Right." I tried again. "I demand a Joke-Off!"

"Crap," said the drake as it slouched. "Just when I was about to have some fun." He glared at me. "You know, it's not like drakes get to do much killing these days. I know I'm only made from dust, but it's the principle of the thing."

"Uhhh…sorry?" I said.

It plodded away as the lights came on.

Standing across from me and Turbo was Rot. He was seated on a little blue throne with a gang of pixies all fluttering around him.

We had obviously found the base of his lair.

"So you want to challenge me?" he said, laughing. "You're just a pathetic knob gobbler. How could you possibly expect to win against the likes of me?"

*Wor—*

"I know, I know," I fumed at myself.

"So you admit it?" Rot asked, eyebrow raised.

"I was talking to myself," I explained.

He squinted.

Then I thought the word *Words* purposefully and heard a ding.

"So, what exactly—" started Rot.

"Stuff it, you tiny rhino tit," I spewed, "or I'll grab your puny ass, shove a firecracker up it, and stick you on a birthday cake."

He nodded slowly while grinning devilishly. "Nice."

"Thanks," I replied, surprised at myself. "So, are you going to accept my challenge or are you too much of a pussy?"

"Oh, I fully accept your challenge, skin flute." He flew down in front of me and glanced at Turbo. "I'm assuming that gonad is going to be the ref?"

"That's right," Turbo spoke up.

He flew in between us as the rest of the pixies all spread out until they formed a circle around me, Turbo, and Rot. They then started chanting for about a minute, building a dome of green light that encased us.

"Okay," Turbo said, clearing his throat. "Here's the deal. Rot, since you were challenged, you get to choose the type of jokes in the Joke-Off."

Rot looked me over, clearly studying me to see if he could spot my style of humor. I wasn't much of a joke-teller, so it really didn't matter which way he went with it.

"Sex jokes," he announced, snapping his fingers. "I remember that his record says he's a real horndog, so I'm guessing he knows at least one or two of them."

Not really. Hopefully this *Words* thing could help me out or I was fucked.

"Wait," I said as the realization of his selection struck me. "If you know I'm a horndog, *why* would you choose sex jokes?"

"He has to, Chief," explained Turbo. "To do otherwise would show weakness."

"Ah." That seemed dumb, but I'd take whatever advantages I could get. "Okay, so now what?"

Turbo held up a finger and looked through the rules again.

"We have to pick what happens when one of us wins," Rot answered for him. "And you call yourself a pixie," he added while shaking his head dreadfully at my pixie. "You disgust me, Turdblow."

"Right," Turbo sighed. "You choose first, Chief."

I nodded. "It can be anything?"

"Yes."

"If I win," I said slowly, "you have to stop doing all your crazy shit, shut down your stupid mob, and surrender."

He shrugged and replied. "Easy enough. And if I win, you have to kiss my balls and then die."

I grimaced.

"What?"

"You heard me, ball kisser," Rot laughed.

"Man," I said, unable to hide my look of disgust, "you guys are some warped little fuckers."

Rot grinned. "Yep."

Turbo turned off his data pad and tucked it into his uniform. Then he raised his hands and started swirling them around, creating a vortex that stood between me and Rot. It was like a tiny tornado made from dark cyan and black. It looked pretty cool, to be honest.

"The challenger will begin with a joke," he announced. "If the opponent laughs, the challenger will be awarded one point. Then the opponent will return the volley with a joke of his own. If the challenger laughs, the opponent will gain a point. The first contestant to reach five points will win the match. Are there any questions?"

I had one: Where the hell was I going to get any jokes that were worth a shit?

But I shook my head instead.

Turbo slashed his hand straight down and called out, "Then let the Joke-Off begin!"

CHAPTER 30

*I* sat there staring at Rot for about a full minute, not saying a word.

*"So,"* I thought directly, *"are you going to give me a joke or what?"*

*"Me?"* replied The Admiral. *"I don't have any jokes, dude."*

*"No, not you. I was talking to* Words.*"*

*"Oookay."*

Suddenly, I felt the desire to speak.

"Uh…" I started strongly. "What's the difference between being hungry and being horny?"

Rot pursed his lips and looked up for a moment.

"Hmmm…what?"

"Where you put the cucumber."

He cracked a smile, but didn't laugh. I nearly did, which made me raise my hand.

"Yes?" said Turbo.

"Am I allowed to laugh at my own jokes or does that give him a point?"

"You may laugh at your own jokes."

"Whew."

145

It was now Rot's turn. I was going to have to clamp down on my emotions here because I tended to giggle whenever presented with juvenile humor. Maybe I had a little pixie in me? Yes, I know that sounded wrong.

Rot leaned in. "Two men were having a drink and one said, 'I had sex with my wife before we were married. What about you?' The other replied, 'I don't know. What was her maiden name?'"

Mmmm…no.

"You'll have to do better than that," I said and then *Words* took over again. "Why does Santa Claus have such a big sack?"

Rot rolled his eyes. "Why?"

"Because he only comes once a year."

The pixie snorted at that and cracked a full smile.

"That counts as a laugh!" exclaimed Turbo while pointing at Rot.

"Damn it." My opponent frowned. "Okay, okay. Uh… What does the sign on an out-of-business whore house say?"

I chewed my lip. "I don't know. What?"

"We're closed. Beat it."

I giggled.

"That evens the score and one to one," said Turbo while giving me the stink-eye.

"What? It was funny!"

But he was right. I had to be careful here. I was in it to win it.

*Words* spoke up. "What's the difference between a G-spot and a golf ball?"

Rot shrugged.

"A dude will go out of his way to find a golf ball."

A bunch of the pixies surrounding us laughed at that, which caused Rot to loose his cool and laugh also.

"Two points to Ian Dex," cheered Turbo.

"Shut the hell up, you guys," Rot jeered at his gang. "Do you want me to win or not?"

He then turned back to me, shaking his head.

"Take your time," I stated coolly.

"Nah," he replied, trying to gain the upper hand. "What do you call a guy with a small dick?"

"Mmmm…Rot?" I answered.

A few of his gang laughed. He didn't.

"Sorry," I said with a bow. "What do you call a guy with a small dick?"

"Just-in."

"Ugh," I said after a moment. It did take some effort, though. *Words* was on deck without pause this time. "What's the difference between a chickpea and a lentil?"

He just looked at me dully.

"I wouldn't pay twenty bucks to let a lentil on my face."

I busted out laughing at that one. He just stared at me for a couple of seconds, looking like he was confused by the joke.

"I don't get…" He paused and then let out a full belly laugh.

"Three points for Ian Dex; one for Rot."

It took a few seconds for Rot to catch his breath.

"Okay, that was pretty funny."

"Thanks," I replied on behalf of *Words*.

Rot flexed his fingers and gave me a stern stare.

"Okay, so a werewolf, a vampire, and a fae are driving along when their car breaks down in front of a farmer's house. They knock on the door and the farmer says they can stay the night as long as nobody touches his daughter. She's smokin' hot, by the way, and she's flirting with the three dudes like it's going out of style."

He leaned back and crossed his arms.

"In the middle of the night, the werewolf says that he's

going across the hall to get him some of that chick. He sneaks over and she's more than willing to take him on."

Rot was really getting into the story now.

"About a minute in, the farmer slams open the door and yells, 'Who is in there?'"

At this point, I was engaged. So was The Admiral.

"Thinking fast," Rot continued, "the werewolf went, 'meow.' The farmer said, 'Damn cat,' and shut the door. The werewolf finished, returned to his room, and told the vampire and the fae how great it was. The fae couldn't resist going next."

I was kind of wishing I had some popcorn right about then.

"About two minutes into the fae's fun fest with the daughter, the farmer pushes open the door and yells, 'Who's in there?' again. Thinking fast, the fae replies with, 'meow.' The farmer slams the door, yelling, 'Goddamn cat!' as he stormed off."

I was already starting to grin.

"The fae finished up and the vampire was already waiting at the door for his turn. He rushed over and started going after it. The farmer's daughter was truly enjoying her evening. Well, about three minutes in, the farmer kicks open the door and screams, 'Who the hell is in there?'"

Honestly, my eyes were wide open at this point.

"The vampire cried out, 'It's me, the cat!'"

After about a minute, I pulled myself back up off the floor only to hear Turbo announce, "That's two for Rot, and three for Ian Dex."

"Nice one," I said, wiping my eyes. "Let's see," I said, nudging *Words* into action. "Okay, so a little boy happens to spy his mother pleasuring herself while moaning, 'I need a man! I need a man!'" He doesn't understand what she's doing, but the next night she has a man over for dinner. Later that evening the mother walks by the kid's room and sees him playing with himself while yelling, 'I need a bike! I need a bike!'"

"That one's older than the crust in your underpants," Rot said without inflection. "What are the three words you *never* want to hear during sex?"

"Mmmm," I said. "I don't know."

"Honey, I'm home!"

I barely even cracked a smile at that one.

*Words* spoke quickly, "You know, my dick was once in *The Guinness Book of Records*…until the librarian kicked me out."

He laughed at that one.

"Four to Ian Dex. Rot still has two. One more and Ian Dex wins the contest."

Rot was looking more than a little concerned at this point. I was just glad to be on the winning side of this battle. If it weren't for *Words*, I'd be kissing the pixie's balls by now.

"What's it called when three people have sex?" he asked.

"A threesome," I answered.

"Correct. What's it called when two people have sex?"

"A twosome."

"That's right, and that's why they call you 'handsome.'"

The Admiral chuckled. Good thing he wasn't playing.

"Nothing?" said Rot. "Jeez. Tough crowd."

*"Come on, Words,"* I said, *"make this one count."*

My eyes flashed.

"A guy gets caught stealing in the Old West. The men who catch him offer him the choice to be hanged or to go through The Test of the Three Tents. He chooses the test. They take him to a hill and point down at the first of the three tents laid out below."

I began to pace back and forth.

"'In that first tent,' one of the men says, 'you will find a bottle of Tequila. You must drink all of it.' The thief nods. 'In the second tent, you will find a tiger with a loose tooth. You must pull that tooth.' The thief gulps but nods. 'In the last tent is the most hideous woman you have ever seen. She's very old, hasn't showered in months, doesn't brush her teeth, and she's downright mean. You have to fuck her.' The thief looks quite disturbed now. 'If you do all three of those things, we'll let you go.'"

I stopped and looked at Rot. He was clearly enjoying this web that I was spinning due to the help from *Words*.

"The thief went down and entered the first tent," I continued. "About thirty minutes later he came stumbling out, barely able to stay on his feet. He took the final swig of the Tequila and threw the bottle on the ground. Then he walked into the second tent."

All eyes were on me at this point.

"The screams and growls were dreadful as the tent bounced around for a good ten minutes. Finally, everything went still. One of the men said, 'Forget it. He's dead.' Just as they were about to leave, another man yelled, 'Wait, he's coming out!'"

I had Rot on the hook.

"The thief stumbled out of the tent, battered and bruised. He had scratches all over him, each pouring blood, and his clothes were nearly ripped to shreds. He looked up at the men on the top of the hill and, in his drunken voice, yelled out, 'Okay, now where's that woman with the loose tooth?'"

Rot lost the Joke-Off.

CHAPTER 31

We stuck Rot in a containment field. Turbo insisted that there was no need for jailing him, but I wasn't taking any chances. While Turbo may be all about adhering to pixie law and protocol, I wasn't so sure about Rot.

I stepped out of the room and held my hands up to the crew.

"We got him and his gang," I explained. "They're not going anywhere." Chuck moved forward, but I stopped him. "Listen, Chuck, I know you want to exact revenge, but we have to get as much information from him as possible first."

"He nearly killed Griff, Chief," Chuck snarled.

"I know," I replied, meeting his gaze, "and you have every right to want to rip him to shreds. But he's the first uber that we've been able to capture. That means he's got information we need in order to prepare for the next uber…or to stop the damn things completely."

Chuck shut his eyes, clearly wrestling with his rage. Finally, he released a long breath and nodded.

151

"You should head back to the hospital and be with Griff," I suggested. "We'll keep you posted."

"And let us know how Griff is doing," Rachel added, stepping up to give Chuck a hug. "We're all thinking about him."

Chuck left the room and I opened the door to take my team into Rot's lair.

Turbo already had all of the pixie gang lined up and ready for processing. They'd be heading to a Netherworld holding cell and sentencing. My guess was that each of them would get a couple of years and a few deep reintegration protocols.

"All right, Rot," I said to the uber who had caused us all this trouble, "I have a few questions and you're going to answer them."

"That wasn't in our agreement," he responded tightly. "I only needed to shut down my mob, stop doing crazy shit, and surrender. There was nothing in your requirements about my answering questions."

"Fair enough," I said with my hands up. "But seeing as how you must stick to the terms of surrender, that means your body is essentially mine to do with as I wish, yes?"

He frowned. "You're not going to make me kiss your balls, are you?"

"Ew," I answered with a sour look. "No. But you injured a member of my team, and his partner is really unhappy about it. In fact, I made him stay out of this room because he wanted nothing more than to rip your limbs from your body."

Rot squirmed slightly, tugging on his collar.

"Now," I continued, "if you don't want to answer my questions voluntarily, I'll just have to ask him to come in here and exact a little revenge on you until—"

"All right, all right," he interrupted while giving me a

disturbed stare. "I don't need the details, shitstain. Ask your fucking questions."

It almost felt like I was sitting in the Directors' conference room dealing with EQK, but this time *I* was in charge. Actually, that thought gave me pause because I really didn't have any designs of being a Director...ever.

"You're an uber," I stated while resting my chin on my hand. "There were a few before you and I'm assuming more are coming. Where are you all originating from?"

His eye twitched and he began to cough.

"I...can't...tell...you...that," he finally managed, and then added, "...jizz pickle."

"Seriously?" I chided. "You can barely talk because of my line of questioning, and you struggle to call me a name?"

He wiped his brow. "It's our way, cock muffler."

I could only thank my lucky stars that we ended up with Turbo in our department and not a pixie like EQK or Rot. Turbo was more my speed, at least on the use of foul language.

"How many more ubers are there?" I pressed.

"No..."

He slumped over, but I snapped my fingers at him, rousing him back awake.

"Answer me, Rot," I demanded. "How many more ubers are there and where are you all coming from?"

"I...I..." His eyes suddenly bulged and he grabbed at his head desperately. "Noooooo!"

The explosion that followed made me glad that we'd put him in a containment field. There was goop and blood all over the place, but at least it wasn't on my suit. Still, I seriously needed to look into magical protection for my clothes, especially my shoes.

"What the hell just happened?" I asked, my jaw hanging slack.

"He blew up," replied Jasmine.

I gave her a look. "Yes, thank you."

Obviously, someone didn't want him to divulge any information. But who? What the shit was going on? My assumption was that there was a lot more to these ubers than I understood.

"So much for that," Rachel murmured. "Well, at least Chuck will be happy that the little creep met his end in a not-so-pleasant way."

"True, but I wish we would have at least gotten some decent information from him first." Then I turned to his gang of pixies. "Do any of you know anything about the ubers?"

They collectively shook their heads that they didn't.

"Figures."

"They could be lying, Chief," Felicia noted.

"Nah," Turbo spoke up. "They've all surrendered, Felicia. Pixies may refuse to answer questions, like Rot tried to do, but they're not likely to lie."

I'll admit that I didn't know as much about pixies as Turbo, but I found it difficult to believe that they wouldn't say or do whatever they had to in order to protect their own butts. Not lie? Come on.

Still, it was also highly likely that none of them knew a damn thing about where Rot came from. He wouldn't have bothered sharing that information with them. To him, they were nothing but peons. A king doesn't confide in peons very often, especially not one bent on destroying anything that stood in his way.

"Well," I said with a heavy sigh, "I guess we're done here. Let's process these guys and get back to base. I need to have another word with the Directors."

CHAPTER 32

The room was silent when I walked in and took a seat. After my last interaction with the Directors, I'm sure they were expecting more of the same angst from me. But I wasn't going to go after them again. There was no point since they wouldn't give me the answers I needed anyway.

"We heard about Officer Benchley," O said, referring to Griff. "I'm assuming he has fully recovered?"

"He'll be fine," I answered. "I have no idea if I'll be able to say that when the next one of my officers falls to an uber, but we all survived this time around."

Okay, so I vented a little.

It quieted the room again.

"We all know how you feel about the latest turn of events, Mr. Dex," Zack said, breaking the silence, "and we wish we could tell you more, but we're just not at liberty to do so at the moment."

"So you said," I deadpanned. "Is there any point in my being here, then, or are we done?"

"We have questions," Silver spoke up, "and I think we'd all appreciate it if you calmed the attitude a bit."

"Agreed, Fangy," EQK chirped. "Cut the I'm-a-big-tough-cop attitude, Dex."

"Shove it up your ass, you little foreskin toucher," I replied without control. "Oh shit," I said, covering my mouth in shock. Clearly *Words* was still lingering in my psyche. That was odd considering those little power words usually didn't hang on that long. "Sorry, EQK...that was...uh..." I didn't want to reveal that I'd been dealing with Gabe. He was the only one who had been helping me out as of late. If they learned about his involvement, they could take him out of the equation, too. "Uh...well...sorry."

"That's the second time you've insulted a superior officer in such a way," O warned. "He is well within his rights to have you formally reprimanded for that."

"Yeah, you sweaty little taint," agreed EQK.

I scoffed and shook my head.

"You know what," I said with a laugh, "go ahead and formally reprimand me. I don't care. He calls me names all the time, but nobody seems to care about that, do they?"

"I'm a fucking pixie, you goat fucker," EQK bellowed. "It's part of my culture to call people names!"

"Yeah?" I shot back in a moment of inspiration. "Well, I'm an amalgamite, and it's part of *my* nature to retaliate when tiny sphincter smudges call me names!"

I had the sense that they were all scrutinizing my words, but I kept my visage stone cold.

"For real?" EQK trilled.

"As far as you know," I answered.

"Hmmm."

"Regardless of your cultural norms, Mr. Dex," O said slowly, "you will show a little respect for the Directors when you are addressing us."

"I was showing a little respect, sir," I answered, keeping my eyes on the spot that EQK inhabited.

"I'm serious," O said in a measured voice.

"Sir," I said, turning to face O, "I will no longer allow myself to be subjected to verbal abuse from EQK, nor should you…at least without the ability to retaliate, of course."

"Listen—"

"Sorry, sir, but no," I interrupted him. "I just spent countless hours dealing with a pixie who put my squad through the ringer. One of my officers was nearly killed, my crew shot and ended the lives of five college-aged normals, and I had to go toe to toe with a pixie in a Joke-Off. I will *not* subject myself to—"

"You fought in a Joke-Off?" EQK interrupted.

"Yes."

"And you won?"

"Obviously, corn hole," I said and winced.

"I'm impressed," EQK said in a voice that sounded shocked. "You've clearly got some skills if you won in a Joke-Off, especially against an uber."

I'd had a fair bit of help, but I wasn't about to tell him that. Fact was that if it weren't for Gabe and his fancy little words, my crew and I would have been dead months ago. Hell, all of Vegas would have been under uber rule by now.

To put a notch in this bullshit "amalgamite culture" thing, I said, "I'm just coming to terms with my abilities in this area. It seems that it's part of who I am."

"Right on," the pixie Director replied. "Fine, then. You can call me names all you want, nipple tongue."

I turned and smiled smugly in the direction of O. He didn't say anything in response, meaning I'd won *this* round.

"What's your plan now?" Silver asked from his side of the room.

"Well, sir, seeing that you all refuse to provide me any

semblance of help, I guess I'll just sit around and wait for the next creature to show up. I'm sure that many people will die, but you have your secrets to keep."

OK, so I wasn't doing very well at keeping things bottled up. They had it coming, though, and their lack of objection to my little outbursts, aside from the name-calling, made it obvious that my assessment was correct.

"Mr. Dex," Silver replied after a moment, "you are in a position of leadership. Therefore, you understand that you can't always share everything with the people who work for you. This is not done because you wish to withhold information, and it's not done because you have any desire to put those people in harm's way. It's done simply because there are things that are on a need-to-know basis."

"Completely agree, sir," I said with a nod.

"Good."

"However, when those who work for me are dealing with a rusty turd hole like Rot, I give them everything they need to stay alive."

"Rot?" yelled EQK, causing me to jump in my chair. "You faced fucking Rot?"

"Yeah," I answered. "Why?"

"Rot's supposed to be dead," he hissed, but I could tell that it wasn't directed at me. "He was supposed to have been killed during the raids. This should not be—"

"Enough, EQK!" admonished O, sounding fierce.

"Fuck you, O," EQK cursed. "You can stick your magic wand up your ass for all I care. The fact that Rot was able to come back—"

"This meeting is over," Zack barked.

The room went dark, leaving me sitting there all alone.

"What the hell was that all about?" I remarked to the empty room.

Obviously EQK knew who Rot was. In fact, I'd go as far

as to say that every one of the Directors knew who he was. This was just like when Zack had a minor personality twitch regarding Rex, though EQK's outburst was more pronounced.

There was damn sure something going on with these guys and the ubers. I just didn't know what it could possibly be.

But I had the feeling that a certain vampire by the name of Gabe might be able to shed some light on things.

CHAPTER 33

*I* was downing a plate of wings and drinking iced tea this time at the Three Angry Wives Pub. Usually I'd get a Rusty Nail, but I had to pick up Rachel from her appointment with Dr. Vernon in a bit, and I wasn't a fan of driving while under the influence.

To be honest, I was a little worried about what Rachel and the good doctor were discussing. Frankly, I was probably even more worried with the possibility that Rachel may haul off and knock Dr. Vernon's block clear from her body. She promised she wouldn't, but I had a feeling that she'd at least be giving Vernon a piece of her mind. I suppose technically that's what you were supposed to do with shrinks.

Griff had been discharged and was home recovering with Chuck by his side. The surgeon said that he'd be allowed back to work in about a week. That would be a pretty impressive healing time for a normal, especially with the size of that bite mark, but for a super it seemed a bit lengthy. According to Chuck, the doctors told him that Rot's pixie dust was laced with a magic inhibitor that thwarted standard healing potions and spells. That damn pixie had been a real

161

piece of work. Fortunately, there had been a specialist at the hospital who happened to be a pixie herself. It took some doing, but she had created an antidote of sorts, explaining it needed time to work.

I glanced up from my plate at the sound of the door opening and spotted Gabe heading my way.

He was wearing a light gray suit this time. It matched the specks of gray in his hair.

Classy.

"Good evening," he said, not even bothering to ask if he could join me. "I hope all is well?"

"Couldn't be better," I replied as I signaled the waiter over. "Bourbon, I assume?"

"Actually, no," Gabe answered. "I think tonight I shall have a martini."

I nodded at him admiringly. Gray suit and a martini?

"You having a midlife crisis or something?" I asked as the waiter walked over. "If you're driving a Porsche, I'm going to be really worried."

He smirked. "I had that a few hundred years ago."

"Ah." I held up a finger at him. "Could you get my pal here a martini, please? It's on me. Oh, and go ahead and bring me the check when you've got a sec."

The waiter headed off.

"Early evening?" Gabe asked, looking at my glass of tea.

"Picking up Rachel in a bit. Don't want to drink and drive, you know?"

"Wise." He studied his fingernails for a moment. "Glad to have her back with you?"

"Definitely better than being apart." I then leaned back and crossed my arms. "So, are you ready to move past our bullshit idle chat and get to the meat and potatoes?"

"I see that *Words* is still running its course," he said with a chuckle. "It may be in there for another day or two.

Unfortunately, any item that connects to your speech centers tends to hang on."

"Super," I said as the waiter dropped off Gabe's drink and the check. "I'm sure that will do wonders for my relationship with Rachel."

I glanced at the bill and dropped a fifty in. Usually I used a credit card, but I didn't want to give Gabe the opportunity to bolt before I did. He had a tendency of splitting before me each time. Paying fast meant I could get out of the building first. It was petty, yes, but I wanted this win.

"The Directors told me what was going on with all these ubers," I lied. "Seems like the jig is up."

He stopped drinking and slowly lowered his glass, looking into my eyes. At first I sensed major apprehension, but then his face softened and a smile filled in. He sniffed and threw back the entire contents of his martini in a single gulp.

"Nice try," he said, not even flinching at the burning the alcohol had to have given him. "I'll admit, you had me fooled for a moment."

Damn.

"So why don't *you* tell me what's going on, Gabe?" I implored, putting my elbows on the table. "You probably know that I nearly lost an officer due to that pixie, yes?"

"Casualties of war," came his nonchalant reply. "It can't be helped, I'm afraid."

"Technically, it *can* be helped if either you or the Directors would give me some basic insights on what's actually happening here."

He stared at me for a few seconds before raising his eyebrows and sighing.

"What would you have me tell you, Mr. Dex?" he asked. "Would you like to know that the next uber will be a vampire or a fae or a djinn? Or maybe it will be another pixie? How would that help your cause?" He looked up thoughtfully. "I'm giving you the means to battle where I can."

"Without an instruction manual," I pointed out.

He shrugged. "Some things you need to learn on your own."

"But why these special word things?" I asked. "How can *that* possibly help me? I'm in the midst of a firefight with these damn beasts and I have to figure out what the hell I'm supposed to do with these extra powers you're giving me. Honestly, how the hell does that make any sense at all?"

He pushed back from his chair and began to stand up.

"Oh, no you don't," I said jumping from my seat and putting a hand on his arm.

He looked down at my hand and then glanced up at me. I took my hand away, feeling like there would be some serious trouble if I didn't. That was strange.

"I'm leaving first," I announced.

Gabe glanced back at the door. "If that makes you feel better, then by all means do so."

"Yeah," I said. "It would."

"Then go."

He looked rather self-satisfied. For some reason, I felt that even though I was trying to gain the upper hand by leaving first, he had effectively just dismissed me. This dude was seriously vainglorious.

"Before you do, though," he added as I turned away, "I would suggest that you be on your guard at all times, Mr. Dex. Poison can strike when you least expect it." He set his coat back on the chair. "It's wise to always have an *Antitoxin* with you."

The word locked in and I rolled my eyes.

"Seriously? You went through all of that so you could try and sneak in the word *Antitoxin*?"

"Don't use it now!" he rebuked.

"I didn't," I said, feeling a sense of pride. "I have to think it a certain way for it to work, Gabe. *That* much I've learned."

"Good," he said. "Good."

I shook my head at him. "You're a real piece of work, you know that?"

He sat down and nodded.

"Yes," he admitted. "I do."

## CHAPTER 34

"*H*ow's everything at base, Lydia?" I asked as I sat inside my Aston Martin while waiting for Rachel. She had gone over her hour by thirty minutes so far. "*Any action?*"

"*It's all quiet, puddin',*" she replied in her sweet digital voice. "*Are you doing okay?*"

"*Yeah, baby, I'm fine. Just a little mental fatigue going on.*"

"*Sounds like you could use a nice roll in the hay with your favorite digital entity,*" she said, giggling.

"*I'm all for that,*" The Admiral piped up. "*Seriously, dude, we need to talk to Turbo about hooking her up with—*"

"*I'll be the first to admit that it'd be tough to keep my hands off you if you had a physical body, Lydia,*" I said. "*Hell, you're probably the only person in existence who'd have a chance at keeping up with me.*"

"*So true,*" she agreed.

That's when Rachel walked out the door and started heading my way. She looked to have a bit of a skip in her step.

JOHN P. LOGSDON & CHRISTOPHER P. YOUNG

I got out of the car and walked to the front to meet her.

"Talk to Gabe?" she asked before I could say anything.

"Yeah. It was pointless." I nodded toward the building. "How was your appointment?"

"Quite good, actually," she replied with a look of surprise. "I have to hand it to Dr. Vernon, she really knows what she's talking about when it comes to relationships."

Uh-oh.

"What do you mean?"

"Well," Rachel started while leaning into me, "she just pointed out how different you and I are."

"Okay?"

"It was a good thing, Ian. Opposites attract and all that."

I squinted. "I wouldn't say we're opposites."

"Oh please," she said while playfully slapping my chest. "You're a horndog who wants variety in the bedroom. I don't mind some, too, but nothing like what you want."

*"She's right,"* said The Admiral. *"That doctor really knows what she's talking about."*

*"Shut up."*

"There's something you're not telling me," I accused Rachel while pushing her back gently. "The doctor suggested something, didn't she?"

Rachel nodded as the corners of her mouth lifted slightly.

"Well?" I pressed.

"She thinks we should have an open relationship."

"What?"

"She thinks it'd be good for us to be able to express our physicality with other people."

"She does, does she?" I said. "Well, we'll see about that."

I started walking toward the building. Rachel caught up and blocked my way.

"Ian," she said, holding me at bay, "I think she's right. You always struggle with being loyal when you're in a relationship, and—"

"*I* do not struggle," I countered. "*You* were the one who fooled around last time we were dating."

Her eyes flashed for a moment, but she took a deep breath and reengaged her calm.

"I'm aware of that, Ian, and I've already apologized for it." She brushed the front of my suit with both hands. "The point is that if you're free to have relations with whomever you wish, then it would release the tension in our relationship because I wouldn't feel the need to be jealous."

I regarded her sanity for a moment. "You *do* realize how stupid that sounds, right?"

"Not to me."

"Okay," I said, aiming for some reverse psychology, "so you'd be totally cool with me heading down to the valkyries and boning all of them, one after the other, in all forms and positions and such?"

"*I'd be cool with that.*"

"*Dude! Shut. The. Fuck. Up!*"

I held up my hand before Rachel could answer.

"Just a quick note that there are *many* of them, and they're *all* gorgeous."

Her eye twitched for a moment, but the smile came back to her face with some effort.

"It's in your nature," she replied. "Hell, maybe I'd even join you now and then."

"*Fuck yeah*," The Admiral bellowed. Then he whispered, "*Uh...Sorry.*"

"For real?" I stammered.

"Sure, why not? You could always join me, too, if I'm with Cletus and Merle or something."

"Ew."

She shook her head and laughed. "Why is it okay for two women to be with a man, but not the other way around?"

"I never said that," I argued. "Just not *my* woman."

"*Your* woman?"

I cleared my throat.

"You know what I mean." I glanced away from her, feeling that this couldn't end well. "Look, you know that Dr. Vernon is only doing this because she wants me to bone her again, right?"

"That's what I thought, too," said Rachel, "until she promised me that she wouldn't lay a finger on you."

That was unexpected. I'd felt certain that the good doctor was just weaseling her way into our relationship somehow. But if she was refusing me access to her personal bits, then maybe she truly was trying to help Rachel and me succeed at this relationship?

But being okay with having sex with others was a big no-no on my list of no-nos.

"I really want to do this, Ian," Rachel said. "I'd rather we share each other than split up again because you have a wandering eye." She pointed firmly at me. "Don't bring up my screwing around again. I already explained how that happened."

"Well," I said, thinking that it *would* be fun to bone those valkyries, "if you're sure."

"*I'm sure*," announced The Admiral. "*Sorry.*"

~

"Honestly," I said, feeling miserable as I sat in the middle of a bunch of naked valkyries, "this has never happened to me before."

"It's okay," Valerie soothed.

*"No, it's not okay,"* whined The Admiral. *"What the hell is wrong with me?"*

*"We're in love, dude."*

*"Oh shit. What did we go and do that for?"*

*"I don't know,"* I answered. *"I don't know."*

~

I got back to my condo and found Rachel sitting on the couch, eating ice cream. She usually did that after an evening of debauchery.

"How were Cletus and Merle?" I asked, not really wanting to know. "Everything good with them?"

"They were great," she said, giving me a wink. "It was a lot of fun."

"That's swell," I said, trying my best not to look gloomy. "I'm glad you enjoyed it."

She tilted her head at me. "What's wrong?"

"Nothing."

"Something's wrong. Were the valkyries all on their periods or something? Their cycles are probably synced after all these years of living together."

I frowned at her. "No."

"Ian?" she said in that tell-me-or-else way she had about her.

My head fell forward and my shoulders slumped. I didn't want her to feel bad about boning Cletus and Merle…. Actually, *yes*, I *did* want her to feel bad about it. But the fact was that we had an agreement. Yes, I was kind of coaxed into it, mostly by my non-functional penis.

*"Hey, go easy, pal,"* The Admiral whimpered. *"I'm feeling pretty down right now."*

*"Appropriate wording."*

*"Nice."*

"Oh, my god," Rachel said, her eyes going wide. "You couldn't do it, could you?"

I stood up straight. "*How* could you know that?"

"Look at you," she said, motioning at me. "Your posture is slouched, you're talking like you just lost your best friend, and I just heard…" Her face went pale.

"No fucking way," I spluttered. "You *can* hear The Admiral!"

It was her turn to slouch.

"I don't believe this! I'm in a relationship with a cock whisperer!"

She grunted and gave me a nasty look.

"Gross."

"Anyway," I said, baffled about all of this. "Yes, I failed in my mission to fuck a bunch of gorgeous valkyries. I couldn't do it, okay?" I put my arms up and gave her an enraged look. "Are you happy now?"

She set the ice cream on the end table and stood up. Then she slowly walked over to me and put her arms around my neck.

"Very," she whispered.

I blinked. "Huh?"

"I never went to see Cletus and Merle," she admitted. "Dr. Vernon said that I should just tell you that so that you wouldn't feel bad about being the only one who was stepping out."

I blinked again. "Huh?"

"I was doing this so that we could stay together, Ian. That's all." She ran her fingers through my hair. "I don't want an open relationship, and now I know for certain that you don't either."

"I…huh?"

She smiled. "Why don't we go in the bedroom and have some fun? Just you and me." She then winked and glanced down at my growing disposition in my pants. "And The Admiral, too, of course."

I said nothing as I followed her dutifully to our love nest.

The Admiral also notably said nothing.

But he did stand at attention.

**Thanks for Reading**

If you enjoyed this book, would you please leave a review at the site you purchased it from? It doesn't have to be a book report... just a line or two would be fantastic and it would really help us out!

*John P. Logsdon*

www.JohnPLogsdon.com

John was raised in the MD/VA/DC area. Growing up, John had a steady interest in writing stories, playing music, and tinkering with computers. He spent over 20 years working in the video games industry where he acted as designer and producer on many online games. He's written science fiction, fantasy, humor, and even books on game development. While he enjoys writing lighthearted adventures and wacky comedies most, he can't seem to turn down writing darker fiction. John lives with his wife, son, and Chihuahua.

*Christopher P. Young*

Chris grew up in the Maryland suburbs. He spent the majority of his childhood reading and writing science fiction and learning the craft of storytelling. He worked as a designer and producer in the video games industry for a number of years as well as working in technology and admin services. He enjoys writing both serious and comedic science fiction and fantasy. Chris lives with his wife and an ever-growing population of critters.

CRIMSON MYTH PRESS

*Crimson Myth Press* offers more books by this author as well as books from a few other hand-picked authors. From science fiction & fantasy to adventure & mystery, we bring the best stories for adults and kids alike.

www.CrimsonMyth.com

Made in the USA
Coppell, TX
06 November 2019